CASE # 4

DARKHILL
SCARY STORIES
HOUSE OF HAUNTS

House of Haunts

by Keith Robinson

Printed in the United States of America
Published by Unearthly Tales on December 2021

Cover design by Keith Robinson

Visit https://www.unearthlytales.com

CASE # 4

DARKHILL
SCARY STORIES
HOUSE OF HAUNTS

a novel by
KEITH ROBINSON

Our Town is Haunted!

Ben, Emma, Nate, and Mia are determined to film the paranormal in the creepy town of Darkhill. They call themselves DARKSEEKERS. And there's an abundance of spooky stuff where they live!

Sinister legends and terrible tales surround the sleepy town of Darkhill, but nobody wants to go on record and say so. "It's bad for business," the mayor insists. "Don't ever talk to reporters."

While most of the residents agree to keep their mouths shut for the sake of the community, a small team of twelve-year-olds are determined to dig deeper into the creepy stories and obtain actual evidence of the supernatural. The brave Darkseekers tackle case after case armed with mobile phones, plenty of enthusiasm, and at least a vague idea of the danger they're getting into.

A ghostly series for fans of Goosebumps, brought to you by the author of the Island of Fog series. These short books are complete stories and can be read in any order.

PART ONE
NATE

Chapter 1
A Risky Mission

Why did I agree to this?

This is what I get for trying to prove I'm not a coward, even though I am. Of all the dumb things I could have said, promising to spend the night in a haunted house takes the cake. The moment keeps repeating in my head—the words spewing from my mouth, everyone looking at me in surprise and telling me how impressed they are, and me realizing what I've done but too chicken to back out . . . I mean, *what the heck?*

It's because of that scary business with the Storm Witch. It shook me up. Mia said I needed to grow a backbone, and everyone laughed, and yeah, I laughed with them—but like an idiot, I got all defensive and tried to show them I wasn't a complete wuss.

"I'll prove it," I told them. "You just wait, guys. Maybe I'll stay the night in the House of Haunts *on my own*. What do you think about *that*, huh?"

Their laughter died. They looked at me, and I gave them all a massive grin—and then realized what had escaped my mouth.

"Gotta say," Ben said, "that'd be impressive."

"Yeah, I'm like . . . *wow*," Mia agreed.

It was all up to Emma. If she could just laugh like it was a big joke, then everyone would join in and I'd be off the hook. I turned to her, hoping she'd pick up on my frantic thoughts. She's usually sharp like that, and kind enough to take pity on me.

But . . . no. She looked at me and said, "You're way braver than me, Nate. So when are you doing this? How about next weekend?"

That was four days ago. It's now halfway through the week, and I'm a nervous wreck.

So yeah, I'd gone from making a light-hearted suggestion to pretty much sentencing myself to Death Row. That's what it feels like, anyway. As the week goes by, the dreaded day looms closer, and I'm finding it harder and harder to concentrate at school.

The House of Haunts scares the pants off me for a few reasons. First, the obvious one—that I'm going to *spend the night in a haunted house*. Second, I'm going to spend the night in a haunted house *on my own*! And third, in order to spend the night in a haunted house, on my own or otherwise, I have to *sneak out in the middle of the night*—and all of this without being caught and grounded for eternity!

So yeah, I'm anxious.

"Not hungry again?" Mom asks me at dinner on Wednesday. "Do you feel okay?"

"Fine," I mutter. "Thinking about the test on Friday."

It's a good excuse, actually. There *is* a test on Friday, and I need a good grade. So I'm trying to study for that as much as I can, if only to take my mind off Saturday night.

"You've been very quiet this week," Dad tells me on Thursday when I fail to laugh at one of his puns. "You all right, son?"

"Sure. Just trying to keep everything straight in my head for the test tomorrow."

"Ah."

On Friday, despite my terror, I ace the test. You'd think a huge distraction like a forthcoming overnight stay in a haunted house would make it impossible to concentrate, but it turns out I'm *so* scared that the test is the only thing keeping me from completely losing it. I've poured all my focus into it as a way to avoid thinking about ghosts, and it's paid off.

"I'm so proud of you!" Mom says that evening when she logs into the school system and sees my grade. "You got a 100, Nate! All that studying, all those quiet evenings in . . . I'm sorry you worried yourself over this test, but what a result!"

I force a smile. "Who'd have thought?"

It's nice that my parents are so happy with my grade. I'm definitely in their good graces tonight. Maybe it'll mean they won't come down on me like a ton of bricks if they catch me sneaking out of the house Saturday night.

Only problem is, now that the test is over, there's no excuse for how quiet I am. And my appetite? Food feels like a sponge going down my throat. But the last thing I need is suspicion, so during Saturday lunch in the kitchen with my mom, I secretly tear bits off my sandwich and feed them to Killer, our German Shepherd. Mom doesn't suspect a thing, and I even go a step further and manage a bag of chips the same way.

"Good to see you eating again," she says with a smile as she reaches for a piece of bread. "Are you seeing your friends today? Now that you're done studying . . ."

"Yeah, we're meeting in Ben's shed."

"Oh?" Strawberry jam drips off her knife as she narrows her eyes and gives me a steely glare. "Now, when you say *meet*, I hope that doesn't mean you're planning to investigate another Darkhill ghost story?"

Argh! I feel so cornered.

"We're always planning that, Mom," I tell her with a smile. Sometimes, honesty works better.

"There's so much to investigate! We're going to be famous ghost-hunters."

"Not at twelve years old, young man. Promise me you won't get into any mischief."

I feign horror. "Mischief? Me?"

"*Promise* me. Leave these horrible tales alone. First you go after a hermit in the woods, then the Gas Mask Kid . . . and then the Storm Witch! She could have killed you all!"

"We weren't investigating a hermit, Mom. We were investigating the Ghost of Direwood. The hermit just happened to be there as well."

The truth about our work as Darkseekers came out last weekend, and all our parents know. That's another reason we've avoided meetings this week. Better to let the dust settle a little.

"No more investigating, Nate," she warns me as she spreads jam on her bread. "It's one thing digging through books and unearthing the secrets of this weird town, but going into dark woods, trespassing on private grounds, wandering about graveyards, knocking on doors trying to find a crazy woman . . . It has to stop. Agreed?"

No! Don't make me promise!

Then again . . . it could be the perfect way to avoid staying the night in a haunted house. What else can I do if Mom directly *forbids* me to get involved in paranormal activity?

Feeling the pressure lift, I'm about to promise I'll never dabble in the supernatural again when her phone rings so noisily it makes us both jump. She answers quickly.

"Beth! I was wondering where you'd got to. So are we going or not?"

I'm holding my breath, that promise still held firmly behind my lips.

She laughs, gets to her feet, and crosses to the window. "I know! I was thinking of getting some more herbs. I love having them ready to pluck for cooking. I used some fresh rosemary in a pork recipe the other day, and oh—just amazing! Are you still planning to pick up potting soil? We can take my car if you want to avoid messing up your squeaky-clean trunk . . ."

I let out a slow sigh. She's completely lost her train of thought about paranormal investigations. It's my chance to slip away before she can finish the call and continue where she'd left off.

Then again, I kind of like the idea of using her as an excuse when the four of us get together in a little while. *Sorry, guys*, I could say with a heavy sigh. *I had it all planned out and was ready to go, but my parents are roadblocking me. If they catch me doing this . . . If I lie and do exactly what they made me promise not to do . . . There's no way, guys. I'm sorry. I'm out.*

The sense of relief that floods through me is incredible. I never fully realized how much stress I've been under this week until this very moment. Sure, it'll be difficult telling the others it's all off, and I know Mia especially will roll her eyes and tell me I'm a chicken. But I don't care anymore. I'm absolutely, definitely *not* spending the night on my own in the haunted house.

And that's final.

****

"Of *course* I'm spending the night on my own in the haunted house," I tell the others about thirty seconds after we start our Darkseekers meeting. "What do you take me for? I said I would, and I'm doing it. I'm ready for this, guys!"

My soul dies inside. Again.

We're in Darkseekers HQ, otherwise known as Ben's dad's shed. A sawdust-covered workbench has tools on it, but otherwise the place is ours to use whenever we want. We're seated around a small coffee table.

"So what time are we heading out?" Mia asks. "We're still riding out there together, right?"

Ben nods. "Yeah. We'll all go to the house, and then the three of us will leave Nate there on his own with the moaning, groaning ghosts."

"And we'll be back first thing in the morning to collect his dead body," Mia adds.

Emma stifles a laugh and reaches across to pat my hand.

"You're all so funny," I mutter. "If there *are* any ghosts hanging about the place, they'd all better quit that moaning and groaning so I can get some sleep."

Mia scoffs. "You? Sleep? Not a chance. I doubt you'll stay more than twenty minutes."

"Ten," Ben cuts in with a smile. "If that."

"Oh yeah?" I lean forward. "We'll see about that. Tonight, then—1:00 AM at the Cold Falls sign. All our parents will be asleep by then."

All three stare at me, and I sense *respect*.

"This is really happening," Ben says softly. "Are you sure, Nate?"

"I'm sure," I growl, one hundred percent the opposite of sure. "It's on, guys."

Chapter 2
Darkhill's Most Haunted House

Creeping out of the house at 12:50 AM is the first step in a night of utter madness. I've snuck out before, and it's pretty easy, but the dread I feel is worse than ever before.

At the entrance to our subdivision, the Cold Falls sign looms in a light mist. It's kind of muggy tonight, like the universe is conspiring to make this event as scary as possible. All I need now is a wolf howling in the distance.

Nobody says a word beyond a muted grunt of acknowledgment. When the four of us are there, all on time, we head out on our bikes with the headlamps off for now. The subdivision is well lit, but we've left it behind now, so the only light we have is the moon. We'll put our lamps on when we reach the back roads, where late-night cops aren't likely to be cruising by.

Ugh. I can't stand the thought of being spotted by Officer Goyles. He'd give a *whoop* of his siren, turn his blue lights on, and report us. We'd be dead by morning, killed by the weighty glares of disappointed and furious parents.

The mist thins as we turn off the main road into Emery Lane. Surrounded by trees on both sides, it's now safe to flick our lamps on. It's highly unlikely anyone will spot us now, except maybe for some cows.

It's a long, twisty lane, but eventually the infamous House of Haunts comes into view. It's the empty home of Bertie Sharpe, an angry old man who died last summer and was buried in Potters Cemetery. He murdered hundreds of people, or so they say. Well, fifty, anyway. At least a dozen. Definitely one or two.

"Did he really kill anyone?" I call to Ben, who always seems to know about these things.

"That's one theory," he says, twisting his head toward me as he rides. "Another is that— Whoa!"

He wobbles and veers sideways, then rights himself. The lane is perfectly clear, but he can't ride properly while looking over his shoulder. When he next speaks, he's facing straight ahead.

"Another is that he had an evil spirit in the house, and he couldn't stop it. Or that he was a ghost himself the whole time."

I have to know. "So which is it?"

Mia chuckles. "He doesn't know, Nate. Nobody does. Lots of stories, no proof of anything."

"But were there bodies? I mean, if people were murdered, there'd be bodies, right?"

"*If* there were murders, maybe," Ben says. He pulls ahead as the slope steepens. His lamp is wobbling all over the place. "But no one found any bodies. No one even looked for them. These are just stories."

"But stories usually have a grain of truth," Emma offers from behind me.

Our conversation pauses until we stop a safe distance from the house, where we can gawk at it in fear—though honestly, all we see in the dark is a grim, hulking blackness. Maybe we'll get a better view when the moon comes back out.

"It's nothing more than an empty house," Ben says. "But Bertie Sharpe lived here for fifty years, and there were stories of people going missing, and they often pointed to him. Once a rumor starts . . ."

Fifty years in Darkhill! It's a strange town, sitting on a hill with forests all around, with so many ghostly happenings that people accept the supernatural as a way of life. Nobody talks about that stuff, and nothing is ever reported in the papers.

That's because the mayor frowns on those who kick up a fuss and bring reporters in from outside. Dad says the mayor wants to 'maintain a sense of normality for the sake of everyone's livelihood'—a veiled threat meaning 'say nothing, or you'll find it hard to make a living in this town ever again.'

So, if there's ever a ghost story in Darkhill, you can bet it's true. I'm surprised Officer Goyles and Officer Deerfoot haven't taken the tales more seriously and dug up Bertie's backyard already!

The moon slides out from behind the clouds, and on a scale of one to ten, my anxiety dials up to eleven. The low roof overhanging the deck at the front is like a giant scowling brow, especially as it sags in the middle. Talk about an angry house! The black windows below are empty eye sockets, but I imagine they glowed a sinister, demonic orange when the old man lived here.

Trees growing next to such an evil place tend to die and look like skeletal hands sticking up from the ground. Well, they do to me, anyway. The creepy mist and distant high-pitched yelp of a coyote are part of the haunted house package. And look at the siding! So old and battered that it's peeling off like flayed flesh. Ivy has threaded and twisted itself up one wall, and I wouldn't be surprised to find it's actually alive, a mass of writhing, slimy tentacles . . .

Okay, stop being so dramatic, Nate.

We ride closer, then let our bikes drop to the ground and stand there for a moment at the foot of the steps leading to the wraparound deck. And it really is a wraparound, literally surrounding the house. The front door is shut, and for a second I pray that it's locked, and that entry is impossible, and we'd all better go on home.

But nope. Ben marches up the steps, tries the doorknob, and pushes the door open. Naturally, the door creaks as it swings inward.

We came to this house not so long ago, a quick trip to show Emma what Darkseekers do. That was a hair-raising experience on its own. I remember seeing a shadowy figure and burning yellow eyes . . . before it vanished into thin air.

"Your adventure starts here," Ben says in a dramatic whisper, gesturing toward the door. "Nate, you're on your own. Enter if you dare."

Mia glances at me. Even in the darkness, I can see the look of scorn on her face. "Oh, Nathaniel, just give it up. We all know you can't do this. Say the word, and we'll all go home."

"Mia, that's enough," Emma says.

I'm grateful that she's sticking up for me, but it's a bit late for that now. Resigned to my doom, I march past the two of them and stamp up the steps to where Ben's waiting on the doorstep. "Y'all need to get off ma porch," I say, attempting an old southern accent. "Go on now, git!"

Ben laughs and grips my shoulder. "Seriously, Nate, are you sure? The phone signal is terrible out here, so you won't be able to call us if you need help."

I watch as he pulls out his phone and thumbs through it. His face is lit up by the screen. Any delay is fine by me, so I wait patiently.

"Yeah, see, no bars at all."

"Well, of course," I mutter. "Whoever heard of a haunted house where you can get a clear phone signal to make calls? How lame is that?"

"There hasn't been phone service since way back at the main road," Mia comments.

Ben glances at my backpack. "Sure you have everything?"

"Yes, Mom." But he isn't checking if I have a change of underwear. In fact, he's asking about our standard-issue paranormal investigation kit. "Cameras, check. Flashlights, check. Candles, check—"

"Snacks?" Mia chips in. "A good book? Stuffed teddy bear?"

"Snacks, check. And comics, actually." It's time to go on in. "Well, see you guys tomorrow."

I shove my way past Ben. Some kind of steely determination is setting in, and I just want to get it over with. My week-long anxiety has led to this moment. The dread, the cold sweat, the lack of appetite, the panic . . . and now I'm here, on the doorstep.

"Go," I tell them. "See you tomorrow."

Ben is silent. The two girls are silent. *Everyone* is silent.

"Go," I say again. "I'll see if I can get some evidence with my camcorder. See you in the morning, bright and early—and I mean *early*, like 5:00 AM, so we can all get back home and into bed before our parents wake."

"Remind me why *we* need to be here in the morning?" Mia murmurs.

"So you know I've been here all night. If I'm going to have a sleepless night, you all can too."

Ben gives me a friendly punch. "All right, buddy, see you tomorrow. And . . . *respect*, man."

A warm feeling sweeps through me, driving away some of my terror. Respect is what I've been hoping for—the chance to prove to my friends that I can be as fearless as them, if not more so.

I watch them depart. It's almost like they're reluctant to go, judging by the way they pick up their bikes and trudge away with them, walking slowly rather than riding off at top speed. They keep looking back and waving as they sink into the darkness. I can barely see them by the time they reach the lane.

My last act before entering is to stash my bike somewhere out of sight. It means coming down off the deck again and hurrying around the side of the house. I'm *really* tempted to just head home. Gripping the handlebars, I resist the urge and park my ride against the deck, nicely hidden in the darkness.

Only then do I return to the deck and approach the door.

This is it.

Taking a deep breath, I step through the doorway. My flashlight is on, and it's wobbling like crazy in my trembling hand. Closing the door behind me is the hardest thing in the world. Now I'm truly alone.

It's like the house has claimed me.

Chapter 3
A Sleepless Night

I have a spare flashlight in my backpack. One just isn't enough. Grabbing the other means I can shine it behind me and prevent any boogeymen from creeping up.

I might have brought too much candy. It takes a minute to rummage through all those chocolate bars to locate the smaller flashlight. Anyway, it's not like I have any appetite whatsoever!

A bunch of candles swim to the surface. Now, where's the lighter? Chasing the shadows away is my top priority, especially since Mia insisted I explore the entire house instead of cowering in a hideyhole. Me? *Cower?* Hmph. She knows me too well. I don't want to poke around in dusty rooms where people were murdered, but if I really must, then I'll brighten the place up as much as I can.

Still trembling, I put all four candles on the floor and light them. I wish I'd brought more, like three thousand of the suckers. But it's enough to conquer the hallway and the staircase. No ghosts lurking anywhere.

"You can do this," I croak under my breath.

Leaving one flashlight on the bottom step and carrying the other, I take a candle through to the next room. Oh, for electricity! To be able to flick switches and flood the house with light . . .

A rocking chair stands to my right. I half expect to find an old man teetering back and forth with a ghastly grin on his face. I remember a comic story with a grandmother who lured kids into a furnace, and she had a creaky rocker, too.

But no, this one's empty. And, thankfully, not moving on its own as it's been known to do.

I *think* this was once the living room. Hard to tell when the house is completely empty. The rocking chair is not Bertie Sharpe's original. It's just a cheap copy, brought in by some joker who thought he could entice a ghost to make it rock.

An opening leads through to what's likely the dining room, because the kitchen comes right after. There are more doors leading back into the hallway. It's a maze around here, each doorway as dark and terrifying as the next.

My heart's thudding like crazy as I move into the dining room and place another candle on the floor. I'm constantly glancing in every direction, certain a ghoul is rushing toward me . . .

That's the hallway and two rooms claimed. Only the rest of the house to go. Why oh why did I only bring four candles?

Because these cheap little things are all that Mom has apart from her more expensive scented candles, and she'd notice if *those* went missing.

Well, maybe two rooms on each floor will be enough. I'll poke around a bit, then find the least creepy place to hunker down for a few hours with my back against a wall. There's no way I'll be sleeping, but I have comics and candy, and a good flashlight with a new battery. I can do this!

Yeah, right.

I return to the hallway, sling my backpack over my shoulder, and head up the stairs. The floorboards squeak loud enough to wake the dead. At the top, I peer along another hallway similar to the one below.

This is the second floor, but I forgot the house actually has three. There's another set of steps at the back end of the house. They're nearly as steep as a ladder, and right above is a pitch-black square opening where possibly a legion of phantoms lurk. Even Mia wouldn't expect me to go up there tonight. Nope. Staying in the house alone is enough, thanks. Nobody said I had to poke around in the attic.

Though trembling like crazy, I'm feeling proud of myself so far. And amazed. This is me, Nate Harmon, on the upper floor of a haunted house after midnight—on my own!

A scrape downstairs sends a jolt of terror up my spine. I breathe hard and shake harder as I edge away from the top step. Funny how it suddenly feels much safer upstairs than down. Who'd have thought?

The scrape comes again, and I swear it's the pitter-patter of running feet, maybe a rodent—no, something bigger, like a coyote. Please let it be a coyote. I'd rather face a coyote than . . . whatever else might be in the house.

Backing farther down the hall, it dawns on me that I'm doing exactly what idiots in horror movies do: not looking where they're going. This is the part where the character rolls his eyes for being so jumpy and spins around—only to find a walking corpse lurching toward him with arms outstretched and fingers curved into claws.

I don't want to spin around. But if a walking corpse is going to lurch toward me, I need to know about it, so I brace myself and pivot, holding my flashlight high.

A shuddering whoosh escapes my lips. There's nothing here. My light jerks about almost on its own until I've covered every nook and cranny.

But there are definitely noises downstairs. A quick scuffling, then soft footsteps, the creak of a floorboard . . .

What would Ben do?

I wish my hands would stop shaking. And my knees are knocking so hard they're probably beginning to bruise.

What. Would. Ben Do?

Be calm. Think. Listen.

An idea occurs to me, and it hits me like a thunderbolt from the Storm Witch's fingers. Maybe that *is* Ben downstairs!

Maybe all three of them are here, feeling guilty about leaving me alone and coming to offer their support.

Could it be them? I have to admit, I'm already feeling a huge wave of relief at the idea they're close by. On the other hand, it also means they don't have a lot of faith in me. That's fair, but it's also annoying. Really? They took pity on me? Came to *save* me?

I'll show them. When they come looking for me, I'll make sure I'm too busy messing with my camcorder to even notice they've arrived.

If it's them.

I hope so, but it's hard to ignore the fact that Darkhill is the most haunted town in the country. It could be my friends . . . or it could be ghosts.

If it's ghosts, they can't hurt you as long as they stay downstairs.

So, ignoring the odd scrapes and bumps, I move down the hall, glancing warily into the rooms off to the sides. The second door is wide open, so it seems like the least risky to pop my head into. The flashlight shows me there's nobody here, but I take an extra moment to shine the beam through the gap by the hinges in case someone is hiding behind the door.

It seems clear, so I edge inside, hoping the door won't slam shut on its own. Another empty, featureless space, probably a bedroom. The drab, faded wallpaper is dry and rippled in places. The floorboards squeak.

Scrawled on the wall opposite the window is a clear message. Placing the flashlight on the floor and pointing it toward the writing, I dump my backpack and search for the camcorder. My hand plunges deep through candy before getting lucky.

"Recording," I whisper. "Okay, guys, so I found these giant words written in blood."

They're not, really, though the words are huge: *LEAVE ME ALONE!*

I can't believe how horror movie-ish this feels. It's almost cliché. Pretty sinister, though, written in large brownish letters and spanning the wall.

"The question is," I continue, keeping my voice low and close to the microphone, "who's it meant for? Was this some ghost telling Bertie Sharpe to leave? Maybe an annoyed caretaker in the past year trying to keep people off private property? Or even some kids having a bit of fun?"

Weird how the sound of my own voice is kind of comforting! I should talk to myself more.

While I'm putting the camcorder back in my backpack, I hear the distinct groaning of creaky boards in another room and sense movement behind me. I freeze—almost literally, because the air just turned cold. This is the part where a head rolls across the floor, or a screaming white-robed woman flies out of nowhere, or . . . or . . .

My heart is thumping hard again, my breath steaming out of my nostrils like I'm locked in one of those cold storage rooms.

But when I turn, there's nothing there. Not that I can see, anyway.

My flashlight is still on the floor. Normally I'd snatch it up and shine it into the corner to make sure it's phantom free. To my amazement, I do nothing, instead fighting the urge to panic.

The cold blast was probably a simple draft.

Yeah, but the window's shut.

Also, most old houses are full of creaks and groans. The building is settling in for the night, cooling off after a warm day.

Except it wasn't all that warm today, was it, Nate? And it's been dark for four or five hours by now, hasn't it?

Yeah, whatever, shut up. The point is, even my own house makes weird noises at night. There are pipes, woodwork, rodents, all kinds of naturally occurring sounds to consider before jumping to the conclusion it has to be ghosts.

My inner voice has nothing to say this time.

By golly, I might conquer my fears after all! I saw a TV show once where a woman got over a lifelong spider phobia by putting her hand in a glass box full of them. She was terrified, but she did it. Instead of yanking her hand away, she battled her terror and stayed put for a good five minutes or more, and those spiders walked all over her arm. Then, after a while, she calmed down, and her fear evaporated.

That's what I'm hoping for right now. I'm not running from the house in terror just because of some icy cold air. I'm standing my ground despite the possibility of a ghost in the shadowy corner, watching me in silence. And the longer I stand here trembling, the calmer I start to feel.

"I'm a Darkseeker," I croak at last, trying to penetrate the pools of darkness. Slowly, I bend to pick up the flashlight and swing it around. To my relief, there's absolutely nobody else here but me. I raise my voice, putting on a more challenging tone. "Come out, come out, wherever you are. You wanna scare me? Go ahead and try."

Fighting talk. Careful what you wish for.

I can't help feeling I bettered myself. At this rate, *I'll* be the one leading the Darkseekers into paranormal situations and facing apparitions head on. Ben, Emma, and Mia will be hanging back while I descend into creepy basements or . . .

Or creepy attics.

The ultimate terror. There's one at the end of the hall. If I can conquer that, then nothing will faze me ever again.

Grabbing my backpack and stepping into the hall once more, I listen for noises. There's nothing right now, so I turn my attention to the steep steps leading up to that awful black hatchway in the ceiling.

You can do this, Nate. You can do this.

Meanwhile, my other inner voice shouts at me to run for my life.

Chapter 4
Into the Attic

I don't know about this.

I'm at the foot of the near-vertical steps, looking up at the ceiling where a square opening reveals nothing but pitch-blackness above. Even when I shine my flashlight up there, it's like the beam is cut off as soon as it enters the attic.

I read a story about that in the Spookies comic: an entity sucking the life out of anyone who came to investigate. Flashlights couldn't penetrate the darkness, which is what made me think of it. The stories in those comics are a bit cheesy, but the artwork is fantastic . . .

Stop delaying, Nate.

I drop my backpack against the wall. I'll need both hands to climb these steps, and the hatchway above is narrow. There's no rail, so I have to grip my flashlight under my arm and cling to the treads. I think there probably *was* a safety rail at some point, but it's gone AWOL.

The moment of truth.

As soon as I stick my head up through the ominous hatchway, I swing my light around as fast as possible, back and forth, this way and that, almost losing my balance in my haste.

Nothing lurches toward me . . . yet.

With the top half of my body leaning into the attic, my legs are now vulnerable to attack from below, so I climb the rest of the way and yank my feet up, then swing my beam around four more times. Still nothing.

Like the rest of the house, the attic is empty. The hatch's square door stands upright, leaning back against one of many angled roof supports.

The entire floor is boarded, which means I won't have to worry about crashing through the ceiling. It's dusty as heck, though. I can see motes swirling in my beam.

"Well, this isn't so bad." My thudding heart gradually returns to normal. "I'm in the attic of the most haunted house in Darkhill—on my own!—at night!—and it's a piece of cake."

Now I wish I'd brought my backpack up with me, or at least the camcorder. I need to prove I did this, and my phone's camera is a bit feeble and grainy in the dark. I could nip down and get it, but would I then have the nerve to come back up again?

They won't believe me if I don't record this. Mia especially. She'll think I hid in a corner on the front deck the whole time.

As I'm standing over the hatch debating with myself, someone shuffles past in the hall below.

The shock of it almost makes me cry out and tumble backward. Instead, I suck in a breath and end up frozen solid, afraid to crouch down for a better look. Whoever that was just now, they've already moved on along the hall.

I'd only seen the top of a bald-headed man and a pair of thick, rounded shoulders. He was hunched forward, shuffling along.

Bertie Sharpe?

If Ben were here, he'd jump down and grab the camcorder. Mia too—and Emma. But me? Nope! I back away from the hatch, losing myself in the darkness of the attic in case the ghost of the old man climbs up.

After bumping my head on a rafter, I sink to my knees and cower for a minute, shaking hard. Yep, it's official: I'm a chicken. And I seriously thought I was getting over my fears? Nuh-uh. If I wasn't in an attic, I'd have bolted three times over by now.

All right, Nate, get a grip. Do you want to sit here quaking with terror all night, or do you want to take control and be a proper Darkseeker?

It takes me a while to steady my breathing. Then, cautiously, I give the attic a quick scan with the flashlight.

Safe. Or safe-ish, anyway.

"I'm not cut out for this," I mumble.

Focus. Look around. The attic's empty, right? You see? Nothing to fear!

Swallowing, I vow to get some of my bravery back. I feel like it's bolted without me.

Come on, Nate, concentrate!

Okay. So . . . there's a circular window in the wall at the far end of the attic, a skylight looking down into the backyard. There's one at the front, too. It's night out, but a faint shaft of light is coming in.

Being careful to dodge rafters, I approach the nearest skylight and press my nose to the glass. It takes a while to figure out where the backyard ends and the woods start. Is that a shed?

It's a summerhouse.

Okay, well, whatever. Turning fully around, I focus on the similar window at the opposite end of the attic. It must look down on the open space out front. Nothing much of interest, then.

Except . . .

Beginning to tremble again, I blink rapidly, hoping I'm only imagining the figure standing in front of that window.

My flashlight is still pointing at the floor. Why won't my arm raise it up? Because I'm paralyzed with terror, that's why. All I can see is a faint silhouette. It might not be a man at all. It could be a coat stand. I'd know soon enough if my arm would just *cooperate* . . .

Sweating and panting, I have to battle my fears and fight the paralysis before I can aim the beam of light ahead of me.

It's not a man. It's a woman. She's standing quite still with her head cocked to one side, a pair of blazing yellow eyes staring at me.

"No, no, no, no, no, no . . ." I croak.

Don't panic, Nate. This is your moment to prove yourself. Be strong. What would Ben do? What would Emma and Mia do? Don't be a chicken all your life! C'mon, man!

I can't believe I'm doing this. I'm pointing my flashlight directly at a ghost! My shaky beam doesn't faze her one bit. She's very posh-looking, wearing a large-brimmed hat, a snug jacket, and a massive bell-shaped skirt that hangs to her feet. Victorian, maybe?

What the heck is she doing in the attic?

I know she's a ghost. I mean, there'd be no doubt even without those telltale burning eyes. The question is, can she hurt me? Is she one of those solid types that can grab my arm and drag me off somewhere? Or just an apparition?

You're doing good, Nate. You're still standing here! Shame you didn't bring your camcorder up.

I'm an idiot. This is prime ghost evidence, and I'm missing it. I do have my phone, though . . .

I drag it out. Grainy footage is better than nothing. My flashlight helps brighten the subject. I keep the beam as steady as my trembling hand will let me, wondering how long I can record this ghost and whether she'll actually show on the screen during playback. It's worked in the past, so my hopes are high.

Then something weird happens. And by that, I mean weirder than a Victorian lady appearing in an attic. There's a flare of light from behind her— from outside the window—followed by a low rumbling, rattling engine. The woman with the huge dress simply vanishes. My beam no longer finds her anywhere even when I scan from corner to corner.

But a quick scan isn't enough. Still recording on my phone, I drill into every nook and cranny with that bright beam. I have to be certain about this. I can't tell the others, "Yeah, there was this ghost, well, I *think* she was a ghost, and she vanished, but I guess she might have ducked down and hid somewhere, I'm not really sure . . ."

Nope. I have to *know*. And I need the evidence on film.

The more I search the attic, the bolder I grow, and the more certain I am that I've just seen a true, bonafide ghost. A Victorian lady in a dress that size has literally nowhere to hide up here.

Good thing you got it on film!

I stop recording and check the footage. Yep, a solid ten seconds of her standing motionless, and another twenty of me searching an empty attic.

Outside, a car door slams. That reminds me of the light and the rumbling engine. Is the car still running? I think it is. Who the heck is here at this time of the night?

I peer through the skylight. But there's too much reflection, so I have to turn both the phone and my flashlight off. Now I can see out.

I don't know what to make of it. An old-style pickup truck is parked outside, its headlamps shining on the house. A curious bright-white mist seems to have sprung up, and a man stands there looking toward the deck at the front.

"Sharpe!" the man shouts suddenly, his words clear even through the glass. "Get out here!"

What the heck?

I wish the man were easier to see instead of just a dark figure in the mist.

"SHARPE! I'm warning you! Get out here now—or I'm coming in!"

Coming in? That's not good.

This is such an unexpected development that I'm completely dumbstruck. Who on earth is he?

The man shakes his fist and yells once more. "I warned you!"

It's at that point I get a good look at him as he stalks around to the back of his rusted, beaten-up truck. He's well over six feet tall, a black-skinned giant wearing a loose, unbuttoned shirt and a white vest beneath, and baggy pants hanging down to clunky boots.

And now he's grabbing an axe from the back of the truck.

"I'm coming in, Sharpe!" the man yells as he heads toward the house. "And if you don't tell me where my wife is, I'm going to kill you right now!"

"No way . . ." I mumble.

Trying to control my shakes, I start recording again and whisper all the details for the benefit of anyone who might later pry the phone from my cold, dead fingers.

As scared and excited as I am right now, the sudden pounding of fists on the front door makes me jump out of my skin. How can they sound so loud? They echo around the house, make the floor shake, and get inside my head. This isn't your normal knocking on the door. No living human can knock that hard.

It has to be another ghost. He's too weird to be anything else. The old-style pickup, the sudden mist everywhere . . .

Over the yelling from outside, a new voice echoes through the house. "Get lost, or you'll be sorry!"

Is that Bertie Sharpe I hear? I never met the guy, of course . . . but who else would answer the call of a furious man pounding on the door?

An event from the past is playing out a couple of floors below.

I *have* to see it.

Chapter 5
Intruder

Armed with a camcorder and a flashlight, I edge along the hallway toward the front of the house. The main staircase beckons. The noise is coming from below, and that's what I have to get on film.

The big man outside keeps banging on the door and shouting.

Bertie Sharpe shouts back, "Get out of here!" Then, in a lower voice, he adds, "Or I'll have to put you in the wall with your wife."

I can hardly believe this is happening. People on the internet talk about quiet, creepy, ghostly occurrences and faint, see-through apparitions. Here in Darkhill, ghosts are far more solid and far noisier. They have their volume turned all the way up. It's unreal how loud the commotion is.

My mind is buzzing so much that it takes me a moment to realize there's a soft yellow glow shining on the wall at the bottom of the staircase. It's not from my flashlight. It's like someone has turned on all the lights downstairs—only there *aren't* any. This house hasn't had electricity for a year. There aren't even any bulbs.

I'm halfway along the hall by now, standing perfectly still while I figure out what the light means. My friends and I have seen this kind of event before, like in the basement of the ruined house in Direwood. It has to be part of a ghostly reenactment, a scene from the past, and it comes with a full complement of visual effects and supporting props. I bet the wallpaper downstairs is clean and bright, like new. Furniture restored, cobwebs and rat droppings swept away, windows washed, floors mopped, the whole shebang.

Meanwhile, the wall directly to my right is badly stained. Yeah, it's still dark and grimy upstairs because the detailed reenactment of the past is for lower-floor spectators only. Which is silly, really, considering there's nobody else here but me. This makes me wonder if ghosts often show up even when there's nobody around to see or hear them . . .

Unless of course Ben, Emma, and Mia are loitering somewhere on the premises. I'm still not sure about that.

Before I can advance any farther toward the stairs, something really weird gets my attention. Weirder than everything else so far, I mean. That stain on the wall to my right is *spreading*. It had started out the size of a football, but now it's twice as big.

Dead center, a hole appears.

It's small at first, just big enough to poke a finger through—not that I ever would. But then the hole crumbles around the edges and widens. I'm both horrified and mesmerized, staring in amazement as bits of the wall trickle loose and scatter on the floor.

When the hole is large enough to get an arm through, it quits widening. That's almost scarier, like the lull before the storm.

The ruckus downstairs has already faded into the background. My full attention is on the hole in the middle of the stain. I recoil from the smell. It's getting stronger, and it's not pleasant. It's like something died inside the wall.

A stream of blood oozes from the hole and down the wall. It's slow at first but picks up speed until it's gushing pretty hard. When it reaches the floor, it pools outward, thick and dark. Of course I step away from it, though for a second I feel almost paralyzed with fear and disgust.

The smell is worse now. I don't have a spare hand to pinch my nostrils—but that reminds me I'm holding the camcorder, and after a bit of fumbling, I start recording and point the lens at the slowly spreading pool of blood on the floor.

My flashlight is wobbling like crazy. And it bounces around even more when a teeming mass of maggots erupts from the hole and spills onto the floor.

"No, no, no, no, no," I moan over and over. It's about all I can manage.

Downstairs, the front door crashes open.

In that brief instant, every drop of blood and every last maggot vanishes. The stain is still right there on the wall, but faded. The hole is nonexistent.

And, strangest of all, *I'm still standing here!*

Of all the unbelievable things to happen in the House of Haunts, this is the most surprising. *I'm still here.* I didn't bolt. True, I'm petrified with horror, but that's to be expected. The point is, I overcame my usual urge to skedaddle.

"I'm da man," I whisper in triumph. I spin the camera to face me and smile into it. "Did you see that? The hole in the wall, and the blood, and the maggots? I hope it wasn't just my imagination. This is evidence, guys—brought to you by Nate Harmon of the Darkseekers. The question is . . . evidence of what, exactly?"

Bertie's words are still buzzing in my head: "I'll have to put you in the wall with your wife." It doesn't take a genius to figure out *this* is the wall he was referring to. The ghastly mess from before wasn't real, merely a ghost's theatrics, but that stain is, like blood has seeped through.

The noise downstairs resumes. It's time to investigate. No more distractions—I must see what all the ruckus is about. The man with the axe has obviously crashed his way in, and it sounds like he's fighting—with Bertie Sharpe!

I have to get it on camera. This is prime-time supernatural viewing. "I'm moving on down the hall, guys," I whisper.

Why am I not more scared? Have I really conquered my fears? I'm still quaking in my boots, and my hands are shaking like crazy . . . but I'm *here*. Heading toward the stairs, toward the danger, instead of cowering in a hideyhole somewhere.

As I arrive at the staircase, two figures come hurtling up toward me. I cry out and back away. Their shadows are enormous—huge, looming menaces cast by the yellow light from below. The two of them are fast, and it crosses my mind that neither is as big as that man with the axe, nor as old as Bertie Sharpe. But before I can process that information—

"Nathaniel!" a girl's voice hisses. "Time to go!"

"Come on! It's getting hairy around here."

I'm still blinking in amazement as they grab my arms. "Mia—Ben—"

"Downstairs, quick," Ben says with a shove that nearly causes me to drop my camcorder.

I stuff it in my pocket, and the three of us start down the stairs. I'm totally befuddled by their arrival. I mean, I'd already suspected they might have come back to the house, but . . .

Nearing the bottom of the stairs, it's fairly obvious we *are* in some kind of reenactment. The wallpaper is clean, the floors are in much better shape, and sure enough, there's electricity! The hall lights are on, and I squint in amazement as we reach the wide-open front door.

"Emma!" Mia calls.

We all pause in the doorway. Emma's standing outside the dining room, her back to us, watching a couple of adults beat each other senseless on the floor.

"EMMA!" Mia shouts.

But Emma can't hear.

"Outside," Ben orders. He practically drags us through the doorway, with Mia protesting on one side and me open-mouthed and silent on the other. It's only when we've stumbled down off the deck that he speaks again. "I'll go back for her. You two wait here."

We're standing in the white mist now, with the rattling engine of the pickup truck nearby, its headlamps flaring.

"Why should *we* wait out here?" Mia demands. "I'm coming in with you!"

Ben turns toward her with a stern look. "*Wait here.* I'm going to drag her away from those . . . those ghosts—"

"No need," I tell him. "She's on her way out."

Emma's chosen the exact right time to flee, because one of the men inside lets out a horrible roar of anguish. I don't think it's Bertie, either. Sounds more like the big man with the axe.

Emma, ducking and covering her ears, runs away from the house and leaps down the deck steps—right into our arms. We clutch her as she cries out and tries to break free.

"Emma!" Ben hisses at her. "Emma, it's us!"

"It's okay," Mia says. "You're safe now. We all are. We're outside, and the ghosts have gone."

They have, too. The house has gone dark and silent. The old pickup has vanished, and the mist has faded.

"Whatever that was," Ben says, leaning close to Emma, "it's gone now. It's okay."

It's amazing how quiet everything is all of a sudden, and how hard I'm breathing.

But what's stranger is how fed up I suddenly feel. I should be relieved that my friends came back for me, that we're all together again—and I am, really. Except they're here out of *pity*. They didn't want to leave me alone. What, leave poor little Nate in a big scary house without his pals?

Well, 'poor little Nate' did great tonight! He has evidence of the paranormal on film! And he'd probably have more if he hadn't been 'rescued' by the other Darkseekers.

"What are you still doing here?" I growl. "You think I can't handle this on my own?"

Emma sighs and shakes her head. "Of course you can. It's just that . . ."

Ignoring Ben and Mia, I step closer to her. "Tell me everything, Emma. Have you guys been hanging around this whole time?"

After a moment, Emma nods.

And she starts at the beginning, from right after we parted ways . . .

PART TWO
EMMA

Chapter 6
Stakeout

"Emma," Ben whispers to me. "Don't just stand there. Let's go!"

I feel bad that we're leaving Nate alone in the house in the middle of the night, but at least we have a plan to watch over him.

We've made it back to the lane. Ben and Mia are busy pushing their way through the hedge. I go to follow, but I'm worried about our bikes.

"We should hide these. What if someone comes along?"

"Who would—?" Ben starts.

Mia heaves a sigh. "The new girl's right. Let's drag 'em through with us."

So, with Mia and I pushing and Ben pulling, we squeeze our rides through the hedge as well. Then I slip through after them.

I think the moonlit field is part of Bertie Sharpe's property, but either way, it's well out of sight of the house behind a thick copse of trees and overgrown bushes. We leave our bikes right there and head across the grass, allowing Mia to lead the way with her flashlight while Ben and I switch ours off. I doubt Nate could see our beams of light even if he were staring out the window right now, but you never know.

"I have to say," Mia whispers, "I really didn't expect Nate to go through with it."

"Me neither," Ben agrees. "I'll give him ten minutes before he comes flying out the door wailing like a banshee."

"Like a what?"

Before Ben can answer, I seize the opportunity to show off my knowledge a little bit. "A banshee is a ghostly woman who wails and shrieks when someone's about to die."

Mia is silent for a moment as we continue our trek. Then she looks back and scowls at Ben. "That's a poor choice of words, then! Wailing like a banshee . . . Like we need to tempt fate like that!"

"Well," Ben argues, "the wailing is for when someone *else* is about to die, so if it were Nate wailing, then he should be safe enough."

"Yeah, but that puts *us* in danger," Mia hisses. "Shut up about wailing banshees."

Ben chuckles, and I can't help smiling. But inside, I'm nervous about this whole adventure. Not only is Nate at the mercy of any ghosts in the house, we're all in real danger of being found out by our parents. If my mom happens to get up to use the bathroom and pops her head in my room as she sometimes does, she'll see I'm not there . . . and then the hysterics will start.

It'll be Armageddon. She'll wake Dad, and they'll run about the house looking for me, then go outside and wake up the neighbors, then put two and two together and start making calls to Mia's and Ben's and Nate's, and then *they'll* be discovered missing, and . . .

"We won't be long," Ben assures me. He's giving me a sideways glance and can apparently read my mind now. "Like I said—ten minutes tops. So, it was fifteen minutes to get here, ten minutes before Nate runs from the house, fifteen minutes home again—that's well under an hour in total. We'd have to be really unlucky for one of our parents to look in and find us missing in that short space of time."

He's right, of course.

The big house looms ahead of us as we emerge from the trees. Mia switches off her flashlight, and we shuffle in the darkness for a while. We're making our way to the rear, where Ben reckons we stand a better chance of spying on Nate without being spotted.

Seeing what looks like a low building directly ahead, Ben points and picks up speed. "Is that a shed? Let's hide there."

It turns out to be a summerhouse, so it's not as enclosed as we thought. That's probably a good thing. I imagine an old shed would be creepy and full of cobwebs.

It's a cute structure, or was a long time ago. It's square with railings on two sides, and a pitched roof supported by four posts. A swing seat hangs in the middle, but it looks filthy, so none of us sit on it. We duck down behind a fence, trying to ignore the mass of dry leaves that might be a nest for all kinds of bugs.

"Like I said," Ben whispers, "ten minutes and we'll be out of here. Just listen for Nate's wailing. I mean yelling."

While Mia hunches over to peer at her phone, Ben and I twist around and study the backside of the house. It's as grim as the front, a hulking structure made up of old, barn-style siding held together with shadows. I can't help shuddering again. And Nate went *in* there?

"I see a flashlight," Ben whispers.

I see it, too, in a downstairs window. Nate's wandering from room to room, and occasionally his beam illuminates the walls, and I can see his outline. He really must be absolutely bonkers to be in there alone.

"Can't believe I made him do this," I mutter.

Ben looks around at me. "It was *his* idea."

"Yes, but you and Mia didn't talk him out of it. And when he looked at me, it was my chance to laugh and say, 'It's okay, we know you're joking, just forget it,' and then he'd have been off the hook. But instead, I asked him *when*."

Mia laughs softly. "Yeah, Emma, that was pretty harsh, I'm not gonna lie. When you said that, I thought, 'Ooh, she's got a heart of stone.' The look on Nathaniel's face when he realized you weren't helping him out of the hole he'd dug for himself . . ."

"Stop! Oh, now I feel awful!"

Ben's laughing as well by now. "Don't worry about it. Look, I'm not saying there are no ghosts in there, because I firmly believe there are, but I'm not too worried. Most of the time, ghosts are scary but harmless."

I can't help snorting. "Harmless? I don't think the Gas Mask Kid was harmless! Seriously, what if something drags him into the underworld?"

"He's upstairs now," Ben says, apparently not listening to me anymore.

I return my focus to the house. Yeah, there's his light, now on the next level up. Most of the house is spread over two floors, but there's an attic as well. I doubt he'll venture up there.

Nate's light goes still, and it's obvious he's put it down. He's silhouetted clearly as he studies the wall with obvious interest. I'm impressed. *Really* impressed. He's actually doing this.

"Huh," Ben says, glancing at his phone. "It's been fourteen minutes now, and no wailing like a banshee."

"No, quite the opposite," Mia remarks. She's watching the house as well, now. "He's putting us to shame. We're out here cowering while he's alone in a haunted house."

"Whoa!" I exclaim, spotting another figure in the room with Nate. "Do you see that?"

But as quickly as the shadow moved into view, it shifts away again. Nate hasn't noticed.

"See what?" Mia asks.

"I . . . I saw someone else just for a second."

Ben and Mia are silent as we scour the house for movement. Nate picks up his flashlight, and then the room goes dim as he moves on.

"Are you sure?" Ben asks me.

"You don't believe me?"

Mia answers for him. "It's not that we don't believe you, but is there a chance you were wrong? Look, it's hard to see, but there's a tree standing between us and the house."

I blink. "There is?"

It takes a bit more squinting to see she's right. It's completely black, a dead, skeletal trunk with a few spindly branches sticking out.

"From where we are," Mia says, "it's standing to the side of that window. Could you have seen the tip of a branch when the wind blew it?"

I can't refute her logic. "I mean . . . maybe?"

"See, this is what being a Darkseeker is all about," Ben says, sounding quite proud. "Not just digging deep to spot ghosts, but looking close enough to figure out what are *not* ghosts." He nudges me. "I'm not saying you're wrong, Emma, but we need to be careful. Don't want to jump at every sound and shout 'ghost!' at every shadow."

He's right about that, but I'm still doubtful of Mia's explanation. There *is* no wind, so it seems unlikely I saw a branch move.

I get to my feet. "Look, I know what I saw, and it wasn't the tip of a branch moving in the wind. I'm getting a cramp sitting here, and it's cold. I'd rather be on my feet and doing something. Plus, I think we should be closer to the house."

"Are you going in?" Mia gasps, apparently thinking I've lost my mind.

"Let's peek in some windows and keep an eye on our friend before the four Darkseekers become three."

With that, I hurry toward the house.

Chapter 7
Spooky Goings-On

Ben and Mia are right behind me by the time I pass the lonely, skeletal tree and reach the back deck.

The house is way creepier up close than from a distance. The deck is fairly solid, but some boards squeak. The screen door hangs loose, resting on the deck and permanently wedged open, and the door itself is slightly ajar. Who knows how many critters have wandered through here over the past year.

I hate how utterly black it is inside. Peering in through the six-inch gap, there's absolutely nothing to see apart from a hint of light in an adjacent room.

Ben reaches past me and pushes on the door. It creaks alarmingly, and he stops. We all freeze, praying Nate didn't hear that. I honestly don't know if he'd be grateful to find us here or angry that we're snooping about on his watch.

"Let's try a window," Ben suggests.

We move along the deck, go around the corner, and stop at the first window. This looks into a room that Nate has claimed with a candle. It's just a soft, gentle, flickering glow, but boy oh boy, what a difference it makes! It doesn't quite chase away the shadows from the corners of the room, but it's clear nobody is in there.

"He should put a candle in every room," Mia whispers.

"He only brought four," Ben tells her. "Four candles, two flashlights, and his phone. And the camcorder. You know, we should invest in some real Darkseeker equipment if we're going to—"

"Shh." Mia sounds cross. "Stop jabbering. He might hear you."

"He's still upstairs," I remind her. "He might hear a creaky door, but I doubt he'll hear Ben's jabbering. Let's try another window."

Mia laughs softly.

We tiptoe around the next corner to the front of the house and pause at another window. The living room? We can see the rocking chair standing there, perfectly still. A candle flickers on the floor.

I try opening the window. To my surprise, it slides up with a soft rasping sound. When the gap is big enough to lean into, I shine my flashlight around to make sure nobody lurks there.

"Clear," I whisper.

Ben stifles a laugh. "You sound like a cop."

"Turn that off," Mia hisses. "Are you guys *trying* to be discovered?"

I switch the flashlight off. But then a scuffling noise causes me to switch it back on and whip the beam around in time to see movement—a black shape in the doorway that darts out of sight.

"There!" I gasp. "You saw that, right?"

Both Ben and Mia saw it just fine. "Okay, that was weird," Ben mutters. "Someone in the hallway looking in?"

I shake my head. "No. I heard a noise inside the room. Whoever that was rushed *out*."

Mia gets started with her logic again. I swear she's trying to one-up me. "Flashlight shadows and noisy rats."

I sigh. "All right, whatever."

I light up every corner of the room to make sure it's empty, then return to the doorway—and realize my beam is projecting into the hallway beyond, fully visible if Nate happens to be close. I snap it off.

And the moment I do so, we all hear that scuffling sound again. It's just inside the window.

We wait, listening intently. Is that the sound a rat makes? I don't think so. I've heard big field mice before, and they make a pitter-patter sound as they run about on their tiny feet. What we're hearing now is more like a *scrape-scrape* noise.

Before I snap the light back on, we hear footsteps in the hallway. Nate must have come back down!

Ben, Mia, and I duck in a hurry when his bright beam approaches. We hunker below the window sill, holding our breath. Nate must be standing in the doorway, trying to figure out what made that *scrape-scrape* noise, assuming he heard it.

We remain frozen, crouching low.

After a while, Nate's footsteps move off.

"That was close," Ben whispers. "Man, he'd kill us if he thought we were spying on him."

We close the window and continue around the house. The front door is open. Did Nate leave it like that? I can't remember.

Making a complete lap of the wraparound deck, we arrive again at the back door. This time, Ben eases it open another few inches with barely any noise, and we squeeze through into a dark, musty kitchen. We stand there absolutely still, shoulder to shoulder.

Hearing soft footsteps above, the three of us huddle together, confused and more than a little scared. So Nate went upstairs again? If so, why's there a flashlight moving in the next room?

Ben, Mia, and I are frozen to the spot. We don't need to discuss what we're seeing and hearing. It's plain as day. There's someone in the house besides Nate. I'm not sure who's upstairs and who's down, but we definitely have company.

Now I'm certain I saw someone earlier when we were hiding in the summerhouse. It wasn't a branch blowing in the wind. It was a person. Or a ghost. Either way, we need to watch Nate's back.

We tiptoe silently through the house, following the moving light. It keeps coming and going, elusive as a will-o'-wisp, a soft glow that fades when we're about to reach it. But, finally, we *do* come across a light—a flickering candle on the floor of the living room. There, in the center, is the fabled rocking chair we'd seen minutes ago from outside the window.

This time it's moving gently back and forth. We stare in astonishment for a good thirty seconds. It continues rocking at a steady speed.

Then the dull creak dies away as the chair slows and becomes still. Ben, Mia, and I remain standing there a while longer, staring at the lonesome chair as though a ghostly figure might rise from it. But there's nothing to see.

Whoever or whatever is down here with us has gone quiet for the moment. I'm certain Nate must be upstairs. We can still hear his footfalls.

"What do you think?" I whisper to Ben and Mia. "Find Nate and split, or what?"

It's almost impossible to see their expressions without blinding each other with our beams, but I think Mia purses her lips and glances upward. "Depends. I mean, Nate will be fine if the ghosts are harmless. I don't want to cut this short just because we got spooked by a rocking chair."

Ben pushes past her. "Hang on a second."

He shuffles closer to the old chair and bends to study it. Then he steps away.

"See that?" he mutters.

Mia and I watch the chair closely.

Abruptly, it starts to rock. Very gently, it moves back and forth and keeps on going.

This is *real*. This is an absolutely genuine haunted chair!

But before I can say anything, Ben holds up a hand. "Look. String."

Mia clicks her tongue and sighs. "Are you serious?"

Striding forward, she inspects the length of string Ben's holding and follows its trail . . . straight to the window. I distinctly remember closing it before, but now it's open maybe half an inch. She yanks the old frame higher and sticks her head out.

Immediately, the sound of laughter floats in. It's the kind of sound I've heard a million times in the school cafeteria.

Ben growls and dashes over for a look. "Sam Davis!" he hisses. "Kaley—and Austin! What are *you* doing here?"

It all comes clear, then. Our rivals! A group of so-called paranormal investigators, hell-bent on messing with us!

I head for the front door, determined to go out there and give them a piece of my mind.

Chapter 8
Visitors

When we'd parted ways with Nate earlier, I was sure he'd closed the front door. Now I know why it's open. A lot of things are suddenly clear, like the second person in the window with Nate, the fleeting glimpse of somebody downstairs, the *scrape-scrape* sounds, the rocking chair . . .

Furious, I hurry outside and around the deck to the living room window Ben and Mia are leaning out of. Sure enough, I almost collide with three other figures as they retreat to a safe distance, wheezing with laughter.

In the back of my mind, our mission tonight is not completely wasted. Not yet, anyway. Rather than yell at the pranksters, I march up behind them and hiss in my fiercest voice, *"What do you think you're doing?"*

To my satisfaction, Kaley actually jumps a mile before spinning around to face me. This causes the boys to laugh harder, and they lean on the railings for support.

"Oh man," Sam says in a high-pitched squeak, "that worked way better than I thought possible!"

"A bit of string," Austin sneers. At least his laughter is under control, unlike the other two giggling idiots. "Some string, a rocking chair, and the legend of a haunted house. So easy!"

Sam's sister, Kaley, has recovered from her moment of fright and seems to be exaggerating her mirth now. I'm not fooled, and I give her an icy glare.

Sam and Kaley Davis—twins, I think—have always enjoyed a cheap laugh at someone else's expense. They're exactly the same at school, always playing stupid tricks like dumping worms and spiders on meal trays, or taping "Kick Me" labels to people's backs, or dropping stink bombs and making fart noises. They're *so* immature.

Austin Meyer is a little different. He's more serious, and I don't know what goes on behind those calculating eyes. I know Ben's wary of him.

There are a few ways to deal with these fools, but I think discreetly is the way to go this time around. It's the only way to save the mission.

I edge closer and lower my voice. "Guys—a word, please?"

Sam's laughter trails off. He's intrigued. Kaley looks uncertain and doesn't approach until her brother does. She pops some gum in her mouth and starts chewing noisily. Austin hangs back, his eyes narrowing with suspicion.

"I'm sure you know Nate is in the house?" I tell them quietly.

All three nod.

"Why do you think *we're* here?" Sam says. "We overheard you all on Thursday during lunch. You got the picture I sent?"

I sighed. "Yes. An unflattering photo of Nate eating noodles. I hope you all had a good laugh."

Sam grins. "Half the school did."

"It explained why he'd been shaking like a leaf all week," Kaley continues. "His plan to visit a haunted house, I mean—not the noodles."

Sam nods. "You guys should learn to keep your voices down if you want to keep secrets."

I grind my teeth. "Okay, so you know we've dared him to be here alone for the night."

"Of course we do," Sam says with a snort.

"And you actually left him here," Kaley goes on. Her eyes are so wide I can see the whites clearly even in the darkness. "Wow."

I shrug. "That's the dare. Wouldn't be much of a dare if we stayed with him."

"Yet you're still here," Austin mutters, coming closer.

"Yeah, well, we had plans of our own to freak him out a little."

I could have told these goons the truth, that we were watching over our friend in case *real* ghosts showed up. But somehow, I think they'd get more of a kick out of a deliberate prank.

That's the thing about these three. They like the *idea* of being paranormal investigators, but apart from the Gas Mask Kid recently, they don't really *believe* what they're investigating. I guess they just haven't delved deep enough yet.

Sam and Kaley share a glance and grin at me. "We're in."

I can hear Ben and Mia arriving, and I forge ahead before they can interrupt. "No, you don't get it," I whisper fiercely. "You're not invited. Too many of us hanging about the house will give it away. We have all kinds of little stunts planned for tonight, and most people would poop their pants. I don't know if Nate will or not, but I don't want to ruin it by having too many of us around."

"What do you have planned?" Kaley asks, so close now that I can smell her chewing gum. "Tell us. We can help."

I shake my head. "Not tonight. Please, guys, let us have this one. We only get one chance. And if it goes well . . . then we'll tell you what worked so you can try it on someone else."

Austin snorts. "How lame. We don't need your ideas. And you don't own the place."

Mia jumps in then, talking casually while she digs out her phone and starts thumbing through it. "Fine. Emma, let's get Nate and go home. I'll call Dad and tell him we're finishing earlier than expected."

Sam's mouth drops open. "Your dad knows you're here? In the middle of the night? And he's okay with it?"

Mia pauses and looks up. "Well, of course he does." She lets her mouth fall open. "Wait—so your parents *don't* know you're here?"

Mia's a genius. I follow her lead and put on an amazed expression as I face the three. "Really? You snuck out here alone? Without saying a word to anyone?"

"Why should we?" Austin mutters, scowling. He still looks suspicious. "So you're saying your parents know about this? They *let* you come out here tonight?"

It's Ben's turn to jump in. "*Let* us? Mia's dad wanted to come, but we persuaded him to stay home. He's waiting for our call, though."

"Don't believe you," Austin mutters.

"Don't care," Ben growls back.

I'm proud of him. He actually looks quite fearless right now, though he's probably quaking inside.

"What kind of dad would let his daughter out at this time of night?" Austin retorts. "I think you're—"

65

"Oh, whatever!" Mia snaps, still managing to keep her voice low. She starts tapping on her phone. "I'm calling Dad. But I warn you—he'll insist on checking in with *your* parents so they know where you are."

"No!" Kaley gasps. "Don't be an idiot!" She makes a grab for Mia's phone, but she's too slow. "Wait a second. If our parents find out—"

"Hey, Dad," Mia says, turning away. I can see her phone is lit up, but I seriously doubt she's talking to anyone. "We're ready to come home. And hey, guess who else is here with us—?"

Sam abruptly snaps a hand up in front of her face, his meaning clear. Mia pauses.

"We're outta here," Sam whispers. "Carry on. We're gone. Don't say a word about us to your dad, or you'll be sorry at school. Hear me?"

There's a tense, silent moment. Then Mia nods and speaks into her phone. "Hey, Dad? I think we need a bit longer. I'll call you back soon, okay?"

When she 'hangs up,' Sam and Kaley can't hustle fast enough. They swing their legs over the deck railing, drop down onto the dirt, and turn to wait for Austin. He of course takes his sweet time, making sure to give the three of us extra-long glares as he muscles past.

"You're liars," he grumbles, pointing directly at us all one by one. "This isn't over."

"Okay," I say with a shrug.

My heart is hammering—not out of fear of these three morons, but because I think we just narrowly snatched a victory. They're actually leaving us alone! And I think Nate's completely unaware, which means we can continue where we left off, only without outside interference.

Instead of heading toward the one and only lane onto the property, Sam, Kaley, and Austin make a beeline for the nearby patch of woods. They spend a moment rummaging around in the bushes to retrieve their bikes, then set off on a trail of some kind. Pretty soon, they disappear into the shadows. Another ten seconds later, their lights come on—faint, flickering beams among the trees.

"Nicely played, Mia," I murmur. "That was a genius move."

"Oh, well, you know . . ." she says, feigning modesty but still looking quite pleased with herself. "I just followed your lead."

My goodness. Mia *complimented* me?

Ben smiles at us both. "Nicely played, both of you. Tonight's mission is saved. Nate still has a chance to run away, wailing like a banshee."

We return to the front door, and I close it softly. The plan is to give Nate plenty of time alone without a bunch of pranksters wandering about and making chairs move. No more false noises or sinister shadowy figures. This time, the house will be silent—unless there are *real* ghosts, of course.

At that moment, the sound of a car's engine carries across the night air, and the twin beams of headlamps play through the trees.

"Uh-oh," Mia whispers.

"Cops?" I wonder aloud. "We have to get Nate out of there—fast!"

"Hold up," Ben says. "It's not the police."

It's hard to see the shape of the approaching vehicle, but Ben's right, it doesn't look or even sound like a police cruiser. It's old and rattly.

"Who *is* that?" Mia murmurs.

The pickup truck—an ancient, squarish, beaten-up piece of junk—rumbles up the lane and takes a slow, lazy arc around the wide clearing in front of the house. The beams dazzle us for a second, but then they move past and light up the front door.

The engine keeps rumbling. Exhaust fumes drift on the breeze. A mist seems to have sprung up out of nowhere, swirling in the bright lights.

"It's busy here tonight," Mia remarks.

I nudge her. "Shh."

Leaving the engine running, the driver gets out. His door creaks as he opens it, and rattles when he slams it shut. He paces back and forth in front of the truck for a while, staring at the house as if trying to decide whether to approach. Then he begins yelling.

"Sharpe! Get out here!"

When nobody answers, the man yells again, louder this time.

"SHARPE! I'm warning you! Get out here now—or I'm coming in!"

Now I'm scared. *Nate's* in there.

"Does he seriously not realize this place is empty?" Mia mutters. "I mean, does it look like anyone lives here?"

"I warned you!" the stranger yells, shaking his fist at the house.

We can't see what he's like except to say he's in his twenties or thirties. He marches to the back of the truck, leans in, fumbles around, and pulls out . . .

An axe.

"I'm coming in, Sharpe!" he yells again as he strides toward the house. "And if you don't tell me where my wife is, I'm going to kill you right now!"

Chapter 9
The Yelling Man

I tug on Ben's arm so hard he winces. "Nate's the only one in there!"

"I *know* that," he hisses back.

I can barely make out his expression in the darkness, but I think he's about as scared as I've ever seen him. And, for once, he can't seem to make up his mind.

"The back door," Mia urges. "Let's see if we can get ahead of this maniac and warn Nate."

She's already taking off before we can reply.

"Mia, wait!" Ben whisper-shouts. He huffs in annoyance, then goes after her. He pauses only to glance back at me. "What are you waiting for? Come on!"

Something is nagging at me. "I'll stay here. Maybe I can distract this guy or something. Just go!"

The stranger has reached the front door by now and is pounding on it. The door isn't locked. Maybe he'll realize that in a second or two.

As Ben hurries off after Mia around the side of the house, I creep along the deck at the front. If this axe-wielding maniac turns his head, he'll see me. But he's intent on kicking and thumping and shouting at the moment.

A voice comes from inside the house: "Get lost, or you'll be sorry!"

It isn't Nate. Nate is probably still upstairs, peeing his pants. Could it be Bertie Sharpe's ghost, then?

Every second this big guy with the axe pounds on the door is a little more time for Ben and Mia to sneak in the back and tear up the stairs to find Nate, or wherever he is at this moment. But when the angry stranger chooses to crash inside, that's when I'll call out to him. I have no idea what I'll say, and I know it'll mean running for my life, but if I can delay him even a few more seconds, that might make a difference.

Something really is nagging at me, though. I can't put my finger on it. It's only partly to do with the man banging on the door. Doesn't he realize this house has been empty for a year? If his wife came here, and he's looking for her, why now? After all this time? Maybe he's got the wrong address.

But there's also the pickup truck . . .

Apart from the dazzling headlamps, it's not much more than a hulking black shape in the darkness. By the meaty sound of its engine, it's a real gas guzzler and reminds me of an old classic. If Ben were here, I'd ask him to pay attention to it. I'm guessing it's from the sixties or earlier.

And there's the bright-white mist, which wasn't there before . . .

My heart has been pounding almost as much as the man's fist on the door, but it calms a little now. I *think* this man isn't real. I think he and his truck are memories from the past. We've seen this kind of realistic reenactment before. The Ghost of Direwood, for one.

He's still yelling and beating on the door, occasionally rapping on it with his axe . . . and he keeps trying the door handle. He grabs it, rattles it furiously, then pounds the door some more.

There's no way Nate locked it. But maybe the owner did back when this incident played out in real life. The pickup truck and its driver are ghosts, and the sinister mist that's sprung up is a dead giveaway.

Ghost or not, the man has lost his patience and is throwing his shoulder at the door. He rams it harder and harder until, suddenly, it gives way and flies inward. He tumbles into the house and resumes his shouting.

"Sharpe! Last chance! Where's my wife? I know you've done something to her! Get out here and talk to me!"

I hurry to the door and peer inside, desperate to keep the man in my sights. He ignores the staircase and stalks toward the kitchen, banging the axe-head against the wall.

I can't help gasping. The place looks different. It looks . . . *clean*. Fresh and new. And there are lights on! I know it's all a vision, but it's still unnerving how real it seems. There's a lamp on a small hallway table, and light shines from under a couple of doors.

"SHARPE" the man yells. "Get out here, you coward!"

He throws open one of the doors, and light floods the hallway. The man disappears into the room for a moment, and he yells some more.

Where are Ben and Mia right now? I assume they snuck in the back and headed straight up the stairs before the stranger broke in. They'll probably appear any second now, with Nate in tow. I want to yell, "The coast is clear!" . . . but that would alert the man.

But what if he *is* a ghost? Will he even hear?

I stand there, frozen and undecided. If this is a ghost, then he can't hurt us. Well, I don't *think* he can. The Ghost of Direwood was like this, real enough to grab Ben's arm and drag him into her house. The Gas Mask Kid, too, had a solid feel about her. So I'm uncertain. What if his phantom axe can do some real harm to the living? I don't want to find out the hard way.

He appears again, stomping out of the room and into the hall. This time he turns his head directly toward me, and I freeze even more—if that's possible. A half-second later, I realize he's not staring *at* me but *through* me. And in that moment, I get my first good look at him.

His skin is black, his hair a little wild, his cheekbones pronounced. He's wearing the kind of clothes I might expect a construction worker or maybe a forester to wear—a thick plaid shirt, baggy jeans, and sturdy boots. And he's carrying the axe, of course. It looks right at home in his hand. It may be wrong to make an assumption, but I think of him as a lumberjack.

He turns away and stomps to the kitchen at the end of the hall. I'm about to breathe a sigh of relief when another man flies out of an open doorway. Both go down in a tangle of limbs and angry shouts, and the axe tumbles clear.

What the heck?

"What did you do to her, Sharpe?" the lumberjack yells.

"You *know* what I did to her, you imbecile," the other man snarls. He's bald and middle-aged. "And coming here over and over isn't going to bring her back!"

My mind is reeling.

I can't get a decent look at the second man, the one who calls himself Bertie Sharpe, but he's obviously small compared to the other. Stocky and strong, he puts up a good fight, lying on his back and trying to squirm free while stretching to reach the axe.

The lumberjack barks inches from his face. "Where's my Matilda? I *know* she's here. I *know* you did something. Tell me, Sharpe, or I'll kill you right now!"

Bertie struggles hard and somehow tips the lumberjack sideways. The big man immediately grabs the scruff of Bertie's shirt, climbs back on top, and shakes him violently.

"WHERE IS SHE?"

"Oh, give it up, you oaf!" Bertie gasps. "You're far too late, my friend. And you're not leaving here tonight. Not this time. I'm just about sick and tired of you and your kind."

You and your kind?

His words send the lumberjack into a rage. I stumble farther backward as he pounds Bertie Sharpe with his fists. To my surprise, the old man starts giggling.

I feel for the open doorway behind me. I don't want to be here anymore, not while these two men roll about on the floor fighting to the death.

The lumberjack is bigger than Bertie Sharpe, and way angrier, so the outcome seems obvious ... although somehow the small, giggling man has managed to grasp the handle of the axe.

I turn and run from the house as a terrible cry pierces the night. It's not Bertie's voice. It's the lumberjack's.

"No, no, no," I moan as I stumble down the steps and away from the house. I'm surrounded by mist, and that mist is lit up by the rattling truck's headlamps. I can't see where I'm going, but it doesn't matter—I have to get away from the horror in the hallway.

Instead, I collide with a small group of people. I recoil and lash out, and hands reach for me, and I spin around and try to run, but they've got hold of me already, and I can't break free.

"Emma!" someone urges. "Emma, it's us!"

"It's okay," another says. "You're safe now. We all are. We're outside, and the ghosts have gone."

Shaking, I blink and gasp and realize the three shadowy figures are Ben, Mia, and Nate. What's more, the mist has lifted, the dazzling headlamps have gone out, and the rattling, rumbling engine must have quit, because all I hear now are the whispering voices of my friends.

"Whatever that was," Ben says, pushing his face close to mine, "it's over now. It's okay."

He's right. The house stands silent. The front door is open, but the hallway is dark. I hear no signs of a struggle from within. Those two men, that fight, the terrible cry . . .

All of it happened many years ago.

Chapter 10
Comparing Notes

"You were *spying* on me this whole time!" Nate shouts. "I *knew* it!"

Ben, Mia, and I share a glance.

"Not *spying*," Ben tells him. "Watching out for you."

"Nathaniel," Mia says, tentatively putting a hand on his shoulder, "we couldn't leave you here alone. It's not that we don't trust you, or we don't think you're capable of spending the night alone, but—"

"I was doing it," Nate snaps. "I was actually doing it! I'm here, at the most haunted house in Darkhill, on my own in pitch-black rooms in the middle of the night, with only a few candles. I went into the attic! I was gonna sleep in this place, guys. I was gonna prove to you that—"

"And you did." It's my turn to interrupt now. "Nate, you're way braver than me. But it turns out the ghosts here are . . . well, real."

Except for all the little noises you heard earlier. Those were probably Sam, Kaley, and Austin, because they were here too, messing about and trying to scare you. But let's save that for another time.

Luckily, Nate's anger seems to fade. He nods thoughtfully. "Well, maybe. Bertie Sharpe walked past while I was in the attic. Then a car pulled up outside, there was shouting, and suddenly there were lights on in the house. I went to look, and the next thing I knew, Ben and Mia were dragging me down the stairs."

"What happened to *you*, Emma?" Ben says, turning to face me. "We called, but you didn't hear us. It's like you were in a trance."

We're standing well away from the house by now, over by the trees where Sam, Kaley, and Austin disappeared earlier. Bertie Sharpe's old home stands silent and dark, as it should.

I sigh heavily and tell them what I saw, in as much detail as I can muster.

Ben nods. "Mia and I caught part of that, but we headed straight upstairs to find Nate. Then ran back down and called for you."

"I didn't hear a thing."

Ben looks thoughtful. "You were mesmerized, caught up in the event. Turns out you saw more paranormal activity tonight than any of us."

Nate puffs out his chest. "Not true. I saw a *ton* of paranormal activity. And heard it. Guys, there was a lot going on tonight. Like, nonstop."

We all hang our heads or look away. I'm glad it's dark where we're standing. The shadows will hide my red face.

I can't see him very well, but I'm fairly certain Nate narrows his eyes at us. "What? What are you . . . ?" He trails off, then puts his hands on his hips. "You know something important. Tell me."

"Nathaniel . . ." Mia starts.

"Don't call me that! Just tell me!"

It's Ben who breaks the news—that our rival gang of paranormal investigators were here in the house, sneaking about and pretending to be ghosts.

"They even had a piece of string tied to that rocking chair in the living room," Ben finishes. "I'm sorry, Nate. We chased them off, but . . ."

"You chased them off," Nate repeats, sounding bitter. Then his tone changes. "You chased them off? How?"

At this, even Ben balks.

I'm thinking, *We told them we were laying traps for you, Nate, to see what would scare you the most. They agreed to leave as long as we swap notes at school.*

Naturally, I keep that part to myself. "Mia was brilliant. She pretended to phone her dad, and she said her dad would call *their* parents as well."

After a moment, Nate smiles. I can see his teeth in the shadows. "That's smart. Nice one, Mia."

"Okay, but look," Ben says, apparently back to Darkseekers business, "the question is, what next? Even with those morons here earlier, messing about, I think it's clear there *are* ghosts in this house. So, do we stay or leave? Honestly, I didn't think we'd be hanging around this long. I figured . . ."

Nate squares off. "Oh yeah? You figured I'd chicken out after twenty minutes and run from the house?"

"Ten minutes," Ben admits.

"Wailing like a banshee," Mia adds.

"Like a what?"

I sigh with impatience. "Never mind, guys. What now? Do we stay or leave?"

Ben is nodding. "I think Nate's proved himself, not that he had to. We should probably get out of here, get home and into bed before our parents find us missing. We can come back tomorrow and investigate some more in daylight."

"Yeah, and we have a bit of useful information now," Mia says, rubbing her chin. "A man comes looking for his missing wife, crashes inside, yells for Bertie Sharpe, threatens him with an axe, and the two have a fight in the hallway—"

"And one of them gets hurt," Nate finishes.

I nod. "Somehow, Bertie got hold of that axe and killed the lumberjack."

Ben is frowning. "So this really happened?"

I blink rapidly at him. "Of course. We all saw the guy arrive in his pickup. This is how ghosts work. They show us the past."

"I know, but . . . Bertie looked quite old in that little reenactment we saw. Did this happen recently? Like, in the past ten years? If so, what's with the old 1950s pickup?"

"Exactly what I thought," Nate says.

They have a point. We all pause to think about that. The timing does seem a bit off.

"As I said, we need to investigate," Mia says. "There has to be something about the murder of this poor man . . ."

She trails off, and we all know why. Darkhill is notoriously bad at reporting stuff like that.

"Well," Mia says with a shrug, "we should get home before—"

"I'm not leaving."

We all turn to Nate. I can't believe those words just escaped his lips. Of all the people to calmly state they want to stick around a haunted house a bit longer, he's the very last person on earth I'd have expected to speak up.

"Nate—" Ben starts.

He holds up a hand. "No. Listen, guys, I know Sam and Kaley and Austin were here tonight, making fake noises and trying to scare me, but I saw and heard stuff that *wasn't* them. Do you think one of those idiots put on a Victorian dress and went up into the attic?"

"Huh?" we all say together.

Nate starts pacing around in a small circle, and I suddenly feel like there's quite a bit he hasn't told us yet.

"Earlier," Nate continues, "when the axeman was banging on the door, I heard Bertie Sharpe say he'd 'put him in the wall with his wife,' kind of under his breath. I think he killed them both."

Mia gasps.

That reminds me of something else. "I heard him say he was sick and tired of their kind."

"*Their* kind?" Mia says with a scowl. "Black, you mean?"

"I don't know," I mutter.

Nate shakes his head. "I don't think that's it. It's something else. I'm not sure what."

"That's not helpful," Ben said with a sigh. "Mia's right. We should leave now and—"

"Bertie said he put her in the wall," Nate says again. "And that can only mean one thing—that he killed the lumberjack's wife and put her in the wall. Maybe him as well."

"Okay, but—"

"So we need to find her. We need to find her bones! You know how this works, Ben. We find the bones, and then the ghosts can rest easy." Nate looks almost crazy now, his eyes bugging out as if he can hardly believe the words spewing from his mouth. "So we go back in there, knock a hole in the wall, find a skeleton, then call the police. Maybe that's all we need to do."

Mia suddenly switches on her flashlight and points the beam directly in his face so he flinches and blinks rapidly. "Are you nuts? Knock a hole in the wall? *Which* wall, doofus? You do realize houses are full of walls, right?"

He bats the flashlight aside. "The one in the hallway upstairs. That's where the blood and maggots spilled out." As if basking in our startled silence, he puffs out his chest again and nods furiously. "Oh yes! The blood and maggots! You think Sam and his sister did that, too? Or Austin? No, I'm telling you, that's where the lumberjack's wife is buried. Her bones are stuffed in the wall. Maybe his as well. And I'm going to find them, with or without you."

He abruptly turns and dashes off toward the house. We're so stunned that it takes a moment to go after him.

"Nate!" Ben hisses. "Slow down! Wait for us!"

We're all running hard by now. Nate is well ahead, no more than a shadowy figure in the darkness, but I swear he glances back as if to check we're following. He probably realizes we'll talk him out of his nonsense if he stands around long enough, so he's moving fast, his limbs outpacing his mind.

"Nate, we'll go in together!" I shout, forgetting for a moment we're trying to be stealthy. "Hold on a second!"

He reaches the deck and climbs the steps. At the open front door, he stops, turns, and stands there a moment.

"We can do this, guys," he announces. "In and out. Smash a hole in the wall, find the body, then get out of here and call the police."

With that, he heads indoors and vanishes into the darkness.

We pound up the deck steps seconds later, but the front door slams shut.

"Idiot," Mia mutters. "I think I like the old Nate better."

She reaches for the door handle, shining her flashlight directly at the door as she pushes it open. The beam leaps inside, lighting up the hall.

There's no sign of Nate.

"Where are you?" Ben calls, giving up the need to whisper. "NATE! Where did you go?"

For a second, I'm fairly sure Nate is messing with us, some kind of payback for being pranked and spied on earlier. But his silence is deeper than that. We stand there in the hallway, listening hard.

"Nate?" Mia says, softly. "Funny, ha-ha, very good. Where are you?"

There's nothing.

No sound whatsoever.

The house is dead.

PART THREE
NATE

Chapter 11
The Dead House

I can't believe I'm doing this—leading the charge into danger! It actually feels good to be the reckless one for a change.

But as soon as I'm through the front door and into the hallway, with my flashlight darting about almost like it has a mind of its own, I stop and realize I'm not *that* dumb. We literally just saw a couple of ghosts fighting to the death in the hallway a few minutes ago. Maybe the four of us are better off sticking together.

I glance over my shoulder. "Okay, so—"

The door slams shut.

It feels like my breath got knocked out of me. Gasping, I jerk the flashlight from side to side. Nobody is lurking in the shadows. Was that the house locking me in, or one of my friends playing games with me? If I'd looked back a nanosecond earlier, I might have seen Ben or Mia or Emma with a grin on their face as they yanked the door shut. But . . . I can't be sure.

Rushing to open it, for a moment there's a resistance when I try to turn the handle. Weird how the axeman had shouldered his way inside earlier, and now there's no damage. Well, I guess not that weird, since it was a vision of the past.

The handle gives suddenly, and I pull the door open. "Guys—" I start.

But nobody greets me on the doorstep.

"Guys?"

There's no sign of them anywhere. How could they have skedaddled so quickly? And . . . why?

They didn't, you idiot, that annoying voice in the back of my head says. *It's the house messing with you. You're in a different time zone now. It's playing a scene from the past.*

Looking around in the moonlight, I have a feeling my inner voice is right. The hard-packed dirt and gravel are a little neater now, less weedy. The deck boards are nailed down. There's an old table and a couple of chairs, complete with a few empty beer bottles and an ashtray. Not exactly a warm, homely feel, but definitely a scene from the past.

Behind me, in the hallway, lights fade into existence. I spin slowly, just in time to see the wallpaper return to its former glory and picture frames appear. Overhead, light bulbs glow so bright they're in danger of exploding.

The front door remains open, but what am I supposed to do? Go find my nonexistent bike and nonexistent friends? I'm in a virtual-reality past, now. They won't be around for years!

I edge back inside the house and stand at the foot of the staircase.

What year is this supposed to be, anyway? As Ben mentioned earlier, the axeman's truck is a 1950s model, although he might not have bought it new. It had looked rusted and beaten-up, so probably a secondhand junker, maybe twenty years old. Still, that puts him in the 1970s. Yet Bertie had looked elderly in the ghostly wrestling match, and in reality, he only died a year ago. He couldn't have been that old back in the 1970s. He would have been fifty years younger!

Speaking of Bertie Sharpe, the man himself is shuffling out of the living room right now. Since the hall light is so bright, I'm completely exposed, standing in plain sight.

Luckily, Bertie heads in the other direction, toward the kitchen. He's *really* old in this vision, unsteady on his feet, and more hunched over. His stocky legs are bowed outward, and he grunts as he hobbles along.

As terrified as I am, for a moment I'm reminded of my old grandfather before he died when I was little. I remember him being just like this—all weak and feeble, complaining about his joints as he shuffled about. According to Dad, my grandfather was 'half the size he used to be.' As a kid I took that literally and imagined he must have been ten feet tall in his younger years.

Slowly, the lights dim. The wallpaper ages rapidly, the picture frames fade away, and the bulbs abruptly vanish. Plunged into darkness once more, my flashlight beam seems to brighten.

I actually preferred living in the past to this creepy emptiness. Now the place is filled with shadows again, and I have to search every corner to make sure nobody is lurking there. What happened? The reenactment is over already?

Backing toward the door, I risk a quick glance over my shoulder. "Guys? You out there?"

No answer. *You're still on your own, Nate.*

Now that all is silent again, I move down the hall and peer into the living room. My light picks out the solitary rocking chair. Everything is back the way it was, and I *think* I'm in the present. But if so, where are the others? Where are my candles, for that matter?

This isn't the present.

Goosebumps prickle my arms. Hairs rise on the back of my neck. I can *feel* the staring eyes, just as I did upstairs when I first walked around. Someone is here.

I spot the pair of glowing yellow eyes before my flashlight gets that far. My beam finds a lanky teenager wearing a hideous sweater and brown pants. He has slicked-back hair, parted with precision.

Then he's gone, almost as though I blinked the apparition away.

"What the . . ." I mumble.

The old me would have run screaming from the room by now. From the *house*. Heck, the old me wouldn't have been here more than two minutes in the first place. But the *new* me . . . As shaky as I am, I refuse to budge. My feet are locked in place, and my flashlight remains aimed at the corner in case the teenager reappears.

He doesn't, and after a while I let out a shuddering sigh. A Victorian woman in the attic, an axeman from maybe the 1970s, and now some guy from—what, the 1940s? This ghost business plays havoc with the nerves! A weak-hearted adult would probably suffer a coronary after spending an hour or two in this place.

To my surprise, I call out into the darkness. "Hello? Anyone there?"

What are you doing? Shut your stupid mouth!

"If someone's here," I continue, defying my inner voice, "please show yourself."

The old me is gone. I seem to have uncovered a deep well of courage. Scouring the room with my flashlight, daring the shadows to come alive, I feel like I'm finally ready. Ready to face a real live ghost head on.

"Talk to me. I want to help."

But my voice echoes around the room and falls on deaf ears. Or maybe *dead* ears.

The rocking chair is unmoving. Funny—I thought it would have been tilting back and forth all evening, what with everything else going on.

There's a thud upstairs. Ah, now it's time for the bumps in the night. Another thud . . . then a series of dull bangs . . . and a muffled dragging sound . . . a harsh scrape . . .

I'm moving into the hallway while listening to this racket. It grows noisier. There's nothing to see on the stairs, but I have a feeling it's all happening out of sight above. I need to go up and look.

The wall. The one with the stain.

That has to be it. This is another blast from the past, when Bertie Sharpe knocked a hole in the wall and shoved a body inside.

My heart is thudding again—*pounding*—and my breaths are ragged. As I trudge up the stairs, it's like my feet are weighted down. There's dim light up there somewhere. Not from an overhead bulb, but a subdued whitish glow.

I can see down the length of the hall well before I reach the upper floor. I pause six or seven steps from the top of the staircase, where the floor is about eye level. Bertie Sharpe is leaning over the motionless body of the axeman.

Bertie's much younger now. Though still bald and wearing the same round spectacles, he's probably in his thirties. He's wearing a casual button-up sweater and brown pants.

The whitish glow comes from both of them. It strikes me as odd to see the ghost of a *living* man standing over the ghost of a *dead* man when, in fact, they're *both* dead. They glow more than I'm used to seeing, which I'm kind of glad about. It's a constant reminder that I'm only witnessing an event from the past, and maybe these two, being less solid, are less likely to physically hurt me.

Bertie heaves the dead axeman upright.

I can't quite see the hole in the wall, but I know it's there. The axe is propped up nearby. Bits of sheetrock litter the floor. One piece is so large it's standing against the opposite wall, like a small door that's come off its hinges.

Though stocky and strong, Bertie still grunts and grumbles as he heaves the corpse into the recess until only the legs are sticking out. Then a struggle follows, because apparently it's a bit of a tight space, and the axeman's legs are long.

"Get in there, Mr. Clydesdale," Bertie gasps. "You should have stayed away, you aggravating man. You should have driven that piece of junk somewhere else and saved yourself—" He pauses and looks upward like he's just remembered something. "Dagnabbit. Now I gotta get rid of that rattling pickup as well."

Mr. Clydesdale. The axeman has a name!

It would be nice to name the others—the Victorian lady in the attic, and the 1940s youth with the hideous sweater.

Rubbing his chin, the bald man leans toward the hole in the wall. "What do you think, Mr. Clydesdale? Think I can get a few bucks for your truck? I know someone who won't ask questions."

He laughs maniacally.

A hand suddenly flops into view and sticks out from the hole in the wall. Not Mr. Clydesdale's hand, though. It's black-skinned but slender. A *woman's* hand.

Bertie Sharpe laughs harder and wags his finger. "Oh, no no no, Mrs. Clydesdale, no way, ma'am. You and your husband are staying put. Reunited at last, eh? Now, both of you be good while I put this wall back together . . ."

I'm standing so still that I'm developing a cramp in my calf muscles. While Bertie replaces the large section of sheetrock, I sidle backward down the stairs, then turn and move a little quicker. The front door beckons.

The reality has hit home. I can't do this alone. We're dealing with ghosts, I get that, but the bodies in the wall—*bodies*, plural—are very, very real. They'll be skeletons by now, of course, but they're still people.

I have to find the others.

And by 'others,' I mean my friends. I have to find my *friends*.

Of course, now that little seed of doubt is firmly stuck in my mind. If Bertie Sharpe is capable of killing two people and concealing them in his house . . .

Does that mean there are others?

Chapter 12
The Others

Before I reach the front door, it slams shut again.

At the same time, it feels like a blast of cold air sweeps through the house. I'm left gasping and shivering, my breath fogging in front of my face. Swinging around with the flashlight, I catch a glimpse of Mr. Clydesdale with his axe, stomping along the hall toward me, and I throw myself against the door in terror.

The axeman is back, and he's very solid and real.

Yeah, now I'm properly scared. If I could bolt, I absolutely would.

I'm trapped. He moves so fast that I have nowhere to go, not even back up the stairs. Fiddling with the door handle and wrenching on it does nothing—the door is jammed shut. I'm plastered flat against it, so all I can do is await my fate.

Mr. Clydesdale marches up to me and stops with this face mere inches from mine. "What have you done with her?" he growls.

Okay, hold on.

Time stops as my mind tries to grasp what's happening here. Mr. Clydesdale is *dead*. He's been dead for decades. Yet he's looming over me right now, shoving his gnarly face toward me, his yellow eyes burning, and he's *talking* to me. Not random words, but an actual question!

"H-huh?" I manage to spit out.

He stares hard at me, then slowly shakes his head. "What have you done with her?"

"Nothing!" I croak. "It wasn't me!"

Mr. Clydesdale slams a fist against the door to the side of my head, and I can feel the impact on the wood. I know for certain he could do some actual damage to me.

"What have you done with her?" he roars.

"I didn't do anything! It was Bertie Sharpe! He killed her!"

I hadn't meant to let that slip, but, you know, I'm wetting my pants here. Cut me a break. The thing is, I would imagine even a long-dead ghost would be horrified at being told his wife was dead.

I'm not sure he heard me, though. "Where's my Matilda?" he angrily demands. "I *know* she's here. I *know* you did something."

"She's . . ."

She's inside the wall with you!

The words dry up in my throat.

This huge man could probably break me in half with his bare hands. He towers over me with a look of fury on his face—but it slowly sinks into my muddled brain that his fury isn't directed at me. This is a remnant, a ghost playing back its final moments, and they don't really know how to act differently. Well, some do. The Ghost of Direwood improvised a bit when we interfered in *her* playbacks. This one, Mr. Clydesdale, is simply rehashing the same old words.

"I *know* you did something, Sharpe," he barks, proving that it isn't really me he's talking to. "WHERE IS SHE?"

"Look, stop yelling!" I squirm out from under his terrible anger. Suddenly free, I scoot away to the other side of the room where I can shout back at him from beyond his reach. "What do you want me to do? Smash a hole in the wall and drag you both out? You're both dead! Do you understand?"

"Matilda," the man says, more softly now. His gaze is fixed on the closed door, and he seems confused that I'm no longer standing there.

Abruptly, like when a TV picture is on the fritz, he flickers and vanishes, then reappears, towering over me, inches away. I jump back with a cry of fright.

His eyes blaze even more than before. What is it with Darkhill ghosts and their yellow eyes?

The next time he speaks, his voice is a little softer. "Where's my Matilda?"

"Okay, *okay.*" My hands are up in a calming gesture. "I think I get it. You're a confused spirit, and you don't know how to communicate with the living, so this is your ghostly way of asking for help. I understand now. Let my friends in, and then we'll go upstairs and . . . and open up the wall. We'll find Matilda. We'll find *you.* And then we'll call the police and give you a proper burial. Is that what you want?"

Mr. Clydesdale's face twists up in rage. I flinch, expecting a blast of noise—but instead, he winks out of existence.

The front door flies open so hard that its small glass panels crack.

My friends are standing on the doorstep.

Emma's the first to speak to me. "Nate! What happened? We came in right after you, and you'd disappeared—"

"So we went around to the kitchen door," Ben interrupts. "No sign of you there, either."

"And the front door was locked when we came back." Mia folds her arms and squints at me. "I assume the ghost of the house did that, rather than you, Nathaniel?"

All their yammering has given me a moment to get over my surprise. I take a slow breath and put on my calmest face. "I was just chatting with Mr. Clydesdale, the axeman who drove up in the truck. Bertie Sharpe killed a woman, Matilda, and when her husband came looking for her, Bertie killed him as well. Both of them are inside the wall. There are two skeletons in there, and we need to uncover them."

I can't help the small satisfaction I get out of their shocked expressions.

Ben licks his lips as he steps inside and peers up the stairs. "Are you sure about this?"

You're seriously asking me if I'm sure?

"I saw it happen," I growl. "I saw the ghost of Bertie Sharpe stuffing the body in the wall. And then a hand flopped out. I'm telling you, they're in there. And all these hauntings . . . They're because Mr. Clydesdale is restless and needs a proper burial. He needs the world to know what happened to him and his wife."

That last bit only came to me in the moment.

Again, a silence. I have to wonder what time it is now. It feels like we've been here all night, but I'm betting only an hour has passed, if that. It would be black outside if not for the moonlight, and it would be just as black inside if the four of us didn't have flashlights. I kind of wish we were in the middle of a scene from the past so we had some of those overhead bulbs working again.

"All right," Ben says with a nod. "The walls are fairly modern, with ordinary sheetrock, so any small hammer will be enough to get a hole started, and then we can rip it apart with our bare hands."

Mia puts her flashlight between her teeth and busily pats her pockets. "Darn," she mumbles at last. "I *wish* I'd brought my hammer."

Emma glances sideways at her. "Do you usually carry one?"

"No, of course I don't."

Ben doesn't look amused. "There has to be something somewhere we can use. A big lump of wood—a brick—even a rock will do."

Suddenly filled with purpose, we all head outside and start scouring the property. I keep my utter relief to myself. I'm playing it cool right now, and I think Emma's impressed. Heck, even Mia is! Ben hasn't said anything yet, but I'm sure he's just distracted.

The best we can find is a loose deck board right outside the front door. I pry it up, give it a twist, brandish it triumphantly, and promptly put my foot through the hole. I go down in a hurry, and the board goes clattering away from me.

Mia laughs as I'm trying to extract myself. "There he is! The clumsy Nathaniel we all know and love!"

Yeah, I feel foolish. But that doesn't stop me retrieving the board and leading the way back inside. It's surprisingly heavy considering it's only about four feet long. It's not a complete board, and the broken end is jagged.

"Let's get this done so we can all go home," I announce.

Chapter 13
Bones in the Wall

Far bolder now that my friends are with me, I stamp up the stairs as if I've been living here for days and know the place inside out. I'm definitely in charge now. For once, it's *me* leading the Darkseekers in a supernatural case. And this one is a doozy! Two dead bodies inside the wall? Two *actual dead bodies*.

The house is as quiet as can be except for our heavy footsteps, the squeaking of treads, and the creaking of the stair rail. There's nobody in the hallway ahead of me.

"It's here," I whisper, my throat suddenly dry. "See this stain on the wall? This is where I saw maggots. A hole opened up, and blood poured out, and suddenly there were maggots everywhere."

"Oh, Nate!" Emma says, one hand flying to her mouth.

"Yeah, it was nasty. Ghosts are so *dramatic*!" I give a quick shrug. "No biggie, though."

"All right, O Brave One," Mia says with a sigh, "how about using that board you're carrying to poke a hole in the wall?"

I pass my flashlight to Emma. All four beams shine on the wall. I notice that Ben has his phone out and has started filming.

Putting all my weight into it, I ram the jagged end of the board against the wall and poke a hole through, then twist and stab until the gap is wide enough to get a whole hand inside.

I don't, of course. Why on earth would I want to do *that*?

We need to yank the sheetrock off, but the idea of putting my fingers inside to get a decent grip fills me with revulsion. What if a skeletal hand reaches for me? Ugh! Cold, bony fingers brushing against my skin . . .

"Here goes," Ben says, thankfully taking my place. He actually sticks both hands inside and turns them palms outward, his fingers taking hold of the sheetrock.

He pulls hard, and a huge section of moldy sheetrock pops off. The lower half of the wall is still intact, but it's easy to look down into the recess between the studs and light it up.

We stare in horror at the grisly sight inside the wall. Two extremely dead bodies, nothing more than dusty skeletons. No bad smell, no rotting flesh, only dried up bones.

"I can't believe this," Emma whispers with her hand clasped over her mouth. "Ghosts aren't a big surprise anymore, but I didn't expect to actually find corpses in the wall!"

"Bertie Sharpe really *is* a murderer," Mia said through gritted teeth. "All the stories about him are true."

Ben is shaking his head. "Oh man, this is bad. Do you know what this means? It means we're going to have to call the police and let them know. And if we call the police—"

"We're as dead as these two," I finish for him. We'd talked about calling the police before, but the reality is different. The idea of my parents finding out we came here tonight scares me more than this creepy old house. "We're done for. No more Darkseeker meetings, no investigating, no nothing. Probably no more sunlight, either. I'll be grounded for eternity after this."

The others seem to share my woes.

"What if we *don't* report it?" Mia mutters.

Ben signs. "We have to, Mia. But we could put in an anonymous call. Nobody needs to know it was us who found the skeletons. It's not that important who found them. The police just need to be told so they can come and take care of it."

"Yeah," Emma agrees, "and the world needs to know what a monster Bertie Sharpe was."

I suck in a deep breath. "Uh, guys? I think I might know what's going on."

Slowly, all three turn to face me, and I squint in their flashlight beams.

"Speak," Ben urges.

Suddenly nervous and feeling like I'm going out on a limb with a crackpot theory, I tell them what's just sprung to mind. "I've seen ghosts here, for sure. We all have. We've even seen Bertie himself. We saw him kill Mr. Clydesdale in the hallway. Only . . . I'm not sure we saw what we thought we saw."

"Seemed pretty clear to me," Emma says.

"We saw them fighting," I continue. "Bertie was casual and sarcastic the whole time, like he didn't care at all, and that's why we all assumed he was a cold-blooded killer. But what if it's not as simple as that?"

They're all staring at me.

"What if," I continue, "Mr. Clydesdale was already dead?"

To my surprise, Mia bursts out laughing. "Well, of *course* he was already dead. That's what we saw in the hallway earlier—two ghosts fighting."

"Yeah, it was a reenactment," Ben says with a shrug. "But it really happened, Nate."

"You're not understanding me. Sure, it was a reenactment—but of Bertie Sharpe killing a *ghost*."

They're staring at me again.

"Bertie Sharpe killed people, for sure," I continue. "But then the ghosts came back to haunt him, over and over. He was probably scared at first, but then he got tired of seeing the same old ghosts showing up time after time, moaning about how they'd been murdered. So, he started *killing* them. Killing them *again*."

"Killing ghosts," Ben says in a monotone as he raises an eyebrow in my direction.

Mia rolls her eyes. "Nate, I think you've lost your mind. You're telling us he spent all his time in this house systematically executing the *ghosts* of people he'd killed earlier?"

"Wait," Emma says, frowning. She looks at me squarely. "Like an exorcist? Banishing demons and dark spirits?"

I want to agree just so I'll have her on my side, but she's not completely accurate. "Um, not exactly. He was a murderer, for sure, and he put those two people in the wall. He was young when he did that. It was probably fifty years ago! But when their ghosts started haunting him, he had a choice—either take the bodies out of the wall and bury them someplace else, or . . . deal with it. So he dealt with it."

"By killing them again and again," Mia says softly. "That's twisted."

"And there are other ghosts here," I add. "A Victorian lady, and a guy with a hideous sweater and bad haircut. I think they're before Bertie's time, but they're still *here*, and he might have had to deal with them, too."

I'm creeping myself out now. But I'm on a roll, putting the pieces together.

"This explains why he looked so old in the reenactment we saw in the hallway downstairs. Because he *was* old. What we saw was Bertie Sharpe attacking the axeman's ghost decades after he actually killed him."

"That's why he mentioned about them coming back over and over," Emma murmured.

"Yes! And that's what he meant when he said he was sick and tired of 'their kind'—meaning *ghosts*. It's why he got mad one day and wrote a huge message on the wall saying 'Leave me alone.' Maybe he thought the ghosts could read— or maybe he just completely lost his mind. Who wouldn't, living in a house haunted by the ghosts of people you've killed?"

Ben, Emma, and Mia continue to peer at me, their flashlights occasionally blinding. Finally, one by one, they start to nod.

"Okay," Ben says. "That's good, Nate. And now we need to figure out what to do about it. Because I'll tell you now, *I'm* not touching a pile of bones!"

And the moment he says that, all hell breaks loose.

We grab each other in fright as, downstairs, the front door and a few windows slam shut. A chorus of mournful cries echoes throughout the house.

With our free hands, we thrust our flashlights from side to side, and the jerking beams catch shadowy figures lurching toward us from down the hall and out of numerous doorways.

"Downstairs!" Ben yells.

We don't need to be told twice. Jostling each other, we practically fly down the banister as five or six dead people reach out for us, their yellow eyes burning.

But there's no chance of racing outside. Nope. Apart from the front door being shut tight, a grim-looking Mr. Clydesdale is standing in the way with his axe, clearly not intending to move anytime soon.

Chapter 14
Phantom Siege

We skid to a halt on the bottom few steps as the man blocking the front door shouts, "Where's my Matilda?"

But there's room for us to avoid him. We make a sharp turn and head along the hall toward the rear of the house. We can go out the back door instead, as long as—

The Victorian lady stands in the way, glaring at us from beneath her wide-brimmed hat. Her voluminous dress billows in a mysterious breeze reserved for the ghost realm.

"I certainly hope you're not trying to avoid paying your debts, Mr. Flannigan."

What the—?

"Try a window," Mia urges.

We all rush into the nearest room. No ghosts! But the window is jammed shut.

"Find something to break it," I suggest.

Yeah, easier said than done when the house is absolutely empty. The only piece of furniture is the rocking chair in the other room, but I can't see us picking it up and lobbing it at the glass.

It looks like Ben is about to launch a kick at it, but Emma yanks on his arm. "*Don't.* You'll cut yourself and bleed to death! There are enough dead people here already."

For a second, we pause and listen. Heavy footsteps on the floor above indicate these ghosts are in a fairly solid state right now. That means we can't just stampede *through* them as we might with the lighter, wispier, see-through variety.

"So many ghosts!" Emma says.

"Who *are* they all?" Ben complains, sounding a little indignant, as if they're messing with his general understanding of how these things work. "There's no way Bertie could have killed them all, is there?"

"He definitely didn't kill that Victorian lady," I whisper. "Bertie's not *that* old. Anyway, she was talking to Mr. Flannigan a moment ago."

"And who's he?"

"Maybe the original house owner?" I suggest.

We move into the next room, tiptoe past the silent, motionless rocking chair, and check to see if the window will open. It's rock solid.

"How about throwing the chair through?" Mia says.

I'd had that very idea earlier! We have to try it. Ben and I pick it up between us and run at the window. I feel a tickle on the back of my hand and panic, thinking it's a deadly spider about to bite me . . . but no, it's just a piece of string trailing across the floor.

We launch the chair at the last second—and despite the terrible noise, it bounces right off the glass and clatters to the floor on its side.

"Huh?" I exclaim. "What, magical glass now?"

Ben absently stands the chair up. "All right, that's not working. Check for a phone signal, guys. We need to call our parents."

"There's no way I'm calling *mine*," I grumble while checking my phone. I'm not sure whether I'm relieved or not to see zero bars.

Nobody has a signal, so we're on our own.

"Ideas?" Ben says, sounding a little hoarse.

We pause to listen for a moment. If this were a small army of living people trying to stop us leaving, they'd be stomping down the stairs by now. Instead, we hear random shuffles and knocks from upstairs—exactly the kind of noises you'd expect from ghosts that go bump in the night. And zombies.

"Let's try other windows," I whisper.

We hurry through the house, our flashlights bouncing around. Mia's the first to shine her light on another phantom lurking by a moonlit window. It's the 1940s teenager with the hideous sweater.

"My father doesn't approve," he complains in a haughty tone.

That's all he says. I'm not sure what his beef is, but we back up.

Then Emma makes a good point. "He's just a snotty kid. There are four of us. Think we can get past him?"

"Better him than Mr. Clydesdale," I tell her, though I'm quaking at the thought of tackling even the most feeble of ghosts.

"On three," Ben whispers. "We split, go around him, yank the window up, and get out."

I see a possible flaw in this plan. "What if the window is stuck like the one—"

But Ben's already counted to three, and he rushes forward with the girls in tow. I leap into action, veering with Emma to the right-hand side of the 1940s boy while Ben and Mia take the left.

The teenager doesn't move, but suddenly two more ghosts are standing by his side, blocking our way. Three pairs of yellow eyes blaze in the darkness.

We skid to a halt.

"I'd say it's faulty wiring," a lanky man says, tilting his head to one side. He's wearing a blue cap with *McIntire Electrical* embroidered on it. "Afraid I gotta report it, Mr. Sharpe."

Ooh, a recent one.

The other newcomer, standing on the left, is a brown-skinned woman with black hair tied in a bun. She's wearing a bright-blue sari with yellow patterns. "I really must insist," she says with a thick Indian accent. "If you do not turn yourself in, then I will have no choice."

We back off, thwarted by the ghostly gang at the window. But her words are interesting. My mind is whirling as we retreat to the doorway.

"These are all people with some kind of complaint," I say in a low voice.

"Yeah, against whoever owned the place," Ben agrees. "We know the most recent owner was Bertie Sharpe. I guess the Victorian woman came to demand payment of some kind from, um—what was his name?—Mr. Flannigan, whoever he is. He might have been the owner a hundred years ago."

"But why was she in the attic?" I mumbled.

"Maybe for no reason whatsoever," Emma says with a shrug. "Theatrics? You know how these ghosts are."

"And the rest of them?" Mia says, sounding doubtful.

Ben is thinking aloud, staring into space. "The electrician had bad news about the wiring, and Mr. Sharpe didn't want him to file a report. The awful sweater guy was about to squeal to his dad about something or other. The lady in blue was about to rat on him . . ."

Mia pinches her nose. "Are we thinking this house has been owned by *one murderer after another*, going back a hundred years?"

That thought gives me the shivers. How horrible! And if that's true . . .

"How many people are buried here?" I croak.

Emma gives a snort. "Count how many ghosts are with us right now. That might give you a clue."

I'm already trying to remember. "There has to be ten of them knocking about the house."

"More than that," Ben says. "We could carry on, room by room, but I'm guessing these ghosts will keep popping up to block our escape."

"Let's try anyway," Mia says. "You go first, Benjamin."

Ben grumbles but takes the lead. Somehow I end up at the rear, which is almost worse.

Over the next five minutes, we complete a tour of the entire floor, and it now seems that every window has a slightly glowing, yellow-eyed ghost standing in the way. There's quite a mixture of people including an early-1900s man wringing a cap in his hands, a pretty woman in a 1950s dress brandishing a closed umbrella like it's a club, a huge black-suited man whose eyes glow eerily from behind dark glasses, and a number of others from various decades past. And of course Mr. Clydesdale by the front door.

My original estimate of ten is low. It's a large house, and we count twelve downstairs, never mind those shuffling around above.

"We're not getting out of here tonight," Emma moans. "What can we do? No phone signal, no weapons, no nothing."

I've never heard her sound so defeated. For once, I'm not the weakest link in our group.

"There's only one thing we *can* do," I tell her, wishing there was an alternative. "We have to get those bones out of the wall."

Although Emma gasps and Ben grimaces, I think each of us knows this already. All these ghosts emerged from the woodwork the moment Ben said there was no way he was dragging a pile of bones out of the wall. The spirits heard him, and they reacted.

"There has to be another option," Ben growls.

I'm glad he's balking. Saves me from doing it.

Mia shines her flashlight in his face. "Maybe we just need to *say* we'll do it. Like, make a solemn promise." She raises her voice. "That's the plan anyway, right, guys? To tell the police?"

Ben nods vigorously and speaks even louder so his voice echoes along the hall. "Yes! As soon as we get out of here, we'll call the police so they can come and start digging up corpses—I mean, start the search and recover the dead so all these poor, tormented souls can be released."

"Yeah!" I add. "That was always the plan. I just wish we could leave. The sooner we get out of here, the sooner we can end this."

Emma remains quiet, but I'm not sure there's much else to say. Crossing my fingers, I sidle toward the kitchen, hoping the Victorian woman has vanished. If so, they probably all have, and we'll be out of here in a heartbeat.

She's still standing there, as real as can be. "I certainly hope you're not trying to avoid paying your debts, Mr. Flannigan."

My heart sinks. Does this mean a promise isn't enough? We're actually going to have to pull those bones out of the wall?

There's no way.

Something rises inside me—a familiar urge to bolt. This time, it's not so much out of fear but desperation. There's a difference. I'm not blindly panicking. I'm talking about a last-ditch effort to escape this place. If I can get out, I can ride until there's a phone signal and call the police. Getting in trouble no longer matters. This is really, really serious.

So I do what I'm good at, and I bolt.

I'm lightning fast, like a squirrel on steroids, darting around the Victorian lady to get to the door. Her movements are slow in comparison. Her arm comes up to block me, her fingers grasping for my collar, and I dodge and duck. Triumph flares inside me, because I'm past her and reaching for the door handle, and she doesn't have hold of me.

Miraculously, the handle gives. That's when the Victorian lady grabs my collar. I'm already halfway out the door when I realize she has me, and her grip is *immovable*, as solid as rock.

Gasping with the sudden pressure around my throat, I thrash and wrench myself from side to side, feeling my jacket tear. I don't care if I have to run stark naked across the fields—there's *no way* I'm giving up now, not when I'm so close to a dramatic escape.

So I wriggle and twist and flail, and suddenly I'm free of my jacket and her grip, stumbling outside and almost falling down. I take off across the backyard, my gaze straight ahead, fully expecting a legion of ghosts to rise from the ground in a glowing mist.

But . . . nothing.

I'm really free!

Chapter 15
Who You Gonna Call?

It's only when I reach the lane that I fully realize my bike is still at Sharpe's house, standing in the shadows around the side.

But obviously the other Darkseekers stashed theirs somewhere. The question is, where? I'm betting nowhere near the house. And it has to be somewhere in *this* direction, toward the lane we rode in on.

There's no phone signal. I seem to remember it quit long before we got near the house, all the way back at the main road. Okay, so I really need a bike.

If I were Ben and the girls, I'd probably shove them through this hedge . . . right about *here.* So I push my way through and let out a whoop of triumph. Yes! A short distance away, a collection of metal frames and spokes gleam as my flashlight picks them out.

Ben's bike will do. I roll it across the grass and through the hedge, switch on the headlamp, then climb on and tear off up the lane.

You're just leaving your friends behind?

I tell my nagging inner voice to shut up. Ben, Emma, and Mia understand I have one mission in mind, and that's to rescue them. They're most likely rejoicing in the fact that I escaped and are at this moment settling down to wait it out, relieved they don't have to extract bones from the wall, knowing it's a matter of time before the cops show up to take over the dirty work. The ghosts can prevent my friends from leaving, but that's about all they can do.

Ghosts are like robots on the fritz, replaying the last moments of their lives. They can't change it up and engage in conversation. All they can do is repeat the same lines over and over, and stand there looking menacing.

Well, they can improvise a little bit. Grabbing my collar, for instance. The Victorian lady never did that when she was alive.

I pause to check for a phone signal. Still no bars. Man, it's 2:30 AM already! Time flies when you're having fun.

It's only when I reach the main road that I finally have a signal. Back in business! I throw the bike down and start pacing, trying to figure out the best way to report this incident to the police. It's not like I can tell them my friends are trapped in the house and a bunch of ghosts won't let them leave. In fact, telling them *anything* about ghosts is a bad idea. It has to be simpler than that, like we came out tonight on a dare and happened to find bones inside the wall.

I tap out 9-1-1 . . . and pause, swallowing and trembling. This call is gonna change everything. Assuming the police believe me and come out to investigate at this time of the night, it'll mean our life as intrepid Darkseekers is over. I can't even imagine how much trouble we'll be in with our parents. We'll definitely be grounded for life.

I have to do this. But . . . my thumb seems to have locked up. It's poised over the green 'call' icon, and I just can't seem to make it operate.

Your friends need you to do this.

I know, I know. But what if it's the useless Officer Goyles on duty, or it's him they drag out of bed and send over? That would be really bad. He despises us and would most likely make calls to my parents and complain a lot before cruising over to the House of Haunts. He might not even bother coming here until the morning.

So . . . I need to make sure it's urgent, like our lives are in danger. But what danger? Should I mention the restless spirits, then?

What's annoying is that the police would get there and find my friends huddled together in a room with absolutely zero sign of anything even remotely paranormal—because ghosts have an annoying habit of vanishing right when you need to prove their existence to others. It's like they're wary of strangers. In movies, ghosts never show up when new people first enter the haunted house. It takes time before spooky stuff starts happening. It'll be the same at Bertie Sharpe's house when the police arrive. The ghosts will mysteriously vanish, leaving my friends sitting there for apparently no reason, looking like complete fools.

The more I think about it, the less I want to call the police.

Who else you gonna call, doofus?

Then it comes to me. I'll readily admit the Darkseekers are too delicate to pull human bones out of a wall—but I happen to know a few people who'd love to get their grubby hands on a real live skeleton or two.

I carefully delete the 9-1-1 digits and switch over to my messenger app. There's a single text from Sam Davis, with a picture he took of me in the school cafeteria earlier this week. I'm staring into space with noodles hanging out of my mouth. He sent this to a bunch of people and kindly included me in his hit list, with the thoughtful message, 'A noodle eating a noodle.'

I'd have come up with a much better caption, but whatever. The point is, I have Sam's number.

I call him, and it rings and rings. Of course he's not answering. It's 2:42 AM. When it goes to voicemail, I hang up and try again. And again.

I'm about to hang up for the third time when, to my surprise, he answers. "Are you tryin' to be funny?" he growls.

"Sam! It's me, Nate Harmon."

"I know, noodle-face. I have your number. I have *all* your numbers."

I falter for a second, wondering why he has all the Darkseekers' numbers and how come we don't have theirs. But that's for another time.

"Want to be a ghost hunter?" I urge. "We found bones in the wall at Bertie Sharpe's house. All the stories are true—he *did* murder people."

"Liar."

"Look, as much as I hate to admit it, we need your help. It's time we came together, pooled our resources, that kind of thing. Can you bring some hammers? Maybe thick trash bags?"

A long pause. "Huh?"

"We need to pull a couple of skeletons out of the wall."

Another pause. I thought maybe Sam would get all excited at this point, but he's annoyingly quiet.

"Are you saying you're still at the house?" Sam says at long last.

"What? Yes, we're still here." There's no point in confusing matters by telling him I escaped. "There are ghosts with us, and they won't let us go until the bones are removed from the walls."

Silence.

Hmm. I'm still not sensing any *excitement*. Maybe I misjudged Sam, or maybe I'm coming on too strong.

"It might not come to that," I tell him. "Maybe all you need to do is show up. I'm hoping you'll scare the ghosts off, and then we can all leave and send the police in the morning."

Then the scoffing starts.

"Yeah, right. You think I'm an idiot, you loser? You think I'm going to crawl out of my bed, find some hammers and trash bags, get on my bike, and come out to Bertie Sharpe's haunted house in the middle of the night to scare off ghosts and dig up bodies? Seriously?"

"Not dig them up, but . . . yeah."

"So answer me this," Sam growls. "Where's Mia's dad right now? Because Mia said her dad dropped you all off at the house. Why haven't you called *him*?"

"Yeah, well, that was all a lie," I admit. "Our parents have no idea we're out."

Sam makes a hissing sound. "I knew it! Austin was right—you lied just to get rid of us. But this stuff about bones in the wall? Being trapped by ghosts? Not buying it, chump."

I grip my phone harder, kind of wishing it was his neck. "And you call yourself ghost hunters? C'mon, man, you know ghosts exist. We all saw the Gas Mask Kid the other week. Austin got burned, remember?"

"Doesn't mean you're telling the truth about Bertie Sharpe's house. Prove it."

And then it dawns on me that I *can* prove it. I tell him to hold on a minute while I sift through some of the video I took earlier. The shorter the better, or we'll be waiting all night for it to send. The clip of the Victorian lady in the attic seems like the best choice. It's thirty seconds in total.

"Sending a video," I tell Sam. "Tell me when you get it."

Sam says nothing. His skepticism is virtually audible. And meanwhile, my friends are probably cowering in some corner with ghosts raging all around them. My patience is wearing thin.

"Sam, have you got it yet?"

"It's downloading," Sam says, sounding bored. Or maybe he's falling back asleep.

I need to keep his attention. "Have you come up with a good name for yourselves yet? If you're gonna be ghost hunters, you need a name. Last time we spoke, you were going to be Haunters?"

After a pause, Sam says, "Austin came up with a better name. We're the Hauntstalkers."

That's actually kind of cool—not that I'd ever admit it. "Hmm. Guess it'll do."

"It's better than Fartseekers."

"We're Darkseekers, not—"

"Shh. Video's playing."

I count to thirty in my head. My timing is pretty accurate; as I reach twenty-nine, Sam lets out a whistle.

"Dude," he says.

A silence follows. "Yes? So you saw her? The Victorian lady in the attic?"

Another pause. Then Sam says, "I did. Could be fake, but . . . Let me send this to Austin and call him. If he answers, we'll have an emergency Hauntstalkers team meeting to discuss it. If there's a majority vote to come and help you, then we'll head out straight away."

"A *team meeting*?" I exclaim. "A *majority vote*? Sam, there's no time for this! Either head out right now, or don't bother!"

"Catch you later, Fartseeker," Sam says with a chuckle, and hangs up.

I almost throw my phone down in anger. What a complete and utter waste of time. I can't expect any help from the Hauntstalkers tonight. What was I thinking?

I need to make a really tough decision: either call the police and face the immense wrath of my parents—or go back to the House of Haunts and drag the bones out of the wall myself.

Two seconds later, I've decided. It's easily the least scary of the two options.

Sliding my phone into my pocket, I grit my teeth and head back to Bertie Sharpe's house.

Chapter 16
Bertie Sharpe

The grim House of Haunts is deathly quiet as I prop Ben's bike against the deck. No movement, no sound, no voices, nothing.

I've been trying to decide whether to sneak in quietly or just throw the door open. Maybe being bold is the answer. In movies, sneaking around at a snail's pace only prolongs the tension and invites sinister figures to lurch out of the shadows. If I'm noisy and brash, maybe I'll startle the ghosts and send them scurrying.

So I stomp loudly up the steps, twist the handle, shove the door open as hard as I can, and blunder inside.

"Hey, guys!" I yell.

Mr. Clydesdale is standing there, holding his axe. "Where's my Matilda?" he roars.

The door slams shut behind me, and the huge man sidesteps to block it.

Well, that's great. Nicely played, moron. You're right back where you started.

I clench my fists. Okay, so the bold approach didn't work. Sneaking in probably wouldn't have, either. Maybe newcomers like the Hauntstalkers or the police would scare the ghosts away, but I guess we'll never know.

Hearing a stampede of feet, I turn to find my friends spilling into the hallway.

"Nate!" Emma says. "Did you call the police?"

All three of them are staring at me with wide eyes, and I suddenly feel like the biggest idiot in history. Swallowing, I shake my head. "Um, no. I couldn't."

Mia's eyes narrow. "No phone service? You ran off without your bike, so I guess you didn't get far enough to—"

"I found your bikes in the field," I interrupt her. "I took Ben's and rode back to the main road. So yeah, I had phone service, and I dialed 9-1-1, but . . . I couldn't place the call. The idea of Officer Goyles waking our parents in the middle of the night, and . . ."

The weight of their stares is making my knees buckle. It doesn't help that an axe-wielding ghost is standing behind me, glowering with his yellow eyes.

"So," Ben says, "you escaped the house, got to safety, and instead of calling the police, you just came back here, knowing you'd be trapped with us until we remove those bones from the wall?"

"Yeah." I hang my head. "Sorry, guys."

After a long pause, the three of them rush toward me. They must be angry. Of all the stupid things I could have—

But all they do is wrap their arms around me.

"Total respect, buddy," Ben says.

"You're a fool, Nathaniel, and we love you for it," Mia chips in.

"I *never* would have been brave enough to come back," Emma adds.

Astonished, I withdraw a little. "Wait, what? You're not mad at me?"

Ben grins. "What's worse than pulling bones out of a wall is the idea of Officer Goyles showing up, and us going home to face our parents. We all got to thinking about it after you escaped, and . . . we're glad you didn't call the police."

I'm startled and relieved at the same time. Still, now we have to face the nasty job ahead of us, and that gives me chills.

"At least the ghosts aren't attacking us," I mutter, glancing back at Mr. Clydesdale, who's still standing there glaring.

"None of them are," Emma says. "They're just blocking the exits. Knocking that hole in the wall upstairs has got them worked up. They're excited, ready to be released, and now they're determined not to let us go until it's done."

"Excited?" I repeat. "Not the word I'd use."

I peer into the nearest room. By the window, another dark figure lurks, its eerie yellow eyes staring at us.

"Well," Ben says, sounding nervous, "now that you're back, and we don't have a team of forensic scientists swarming the place, I guess we'll have to go upstairs and get this done."

"Is it even legal to mess with those bones?" Mia grumbles.

"Maybe we don't need to remove all of them," I offer. "Just one or two, so it's like a promise?"

"A token of goodwill," Emma says with a nod. "I like it."

We're about to head on upstairs when we hear something. We all pause, listening hard. What *is* that? A soft, rhythmic creaking sound . . .

A moment later, we identify the source of the noise and edge into the living room. The solitary chair we'd tried to throw out the window earlier is back in the center, rocking gently.

Sitting in the chair is Bertie Sharpe.

He's completely solid and real, and if we didn't already know he died a year ago, I'd swear he'd come home. But when he looks up briefly, his eyes give him away—the usual spooky yellow glow. I'm guessing he's about as old as he ever was in life. This has to be an apparition from his last year or so, maybe even his last few months.

On his lap is what looks like a journal. He has a badly chewed pen in one hand, and he's slowly scrawling a new entry.

"That's it," he mutters, putting the pen down. "That's the last one. I'm finished."

He slips the pen into his shirt pocket, then gently closes the book. After a few thoughtful nods, he sighs, leans forward, and eases himself out of the rocking chair.

It's only then I notice a patch of rug under his feet. It's not the complete rug, merely a circular apparition a little wider than the chair, fading to invisibility at the edges.

Bertie grasps his lower back and straightens up with a groan. He has the journal grasped in his other hand as he hobbles slowly toward us. Underfoot, the edge of the rug comes into view. It's like he's pointing a flashlight at the floor as he walks, and instead of a beam of light, we're seeing a projection of the past.

Silently, Ben and Emma move to one side, Mia and I to the other. Bertie Sharpe passes between us all, close enough to touch.

We've seen plenty of ghosts now, and we know this one isn't about to lash out. This is a vision, and we need to see it through. So we shuffle after the old man as he heads slowly along the hall toward the front door.

Mr. Clydesdale glares at him but makes no move. The weirdness of it is mind-boggling. These spirits co-exist with an intense dislike of each other. I wonder if Bertie even knows he's ended up here with the rest.

Slowly, the elderly man climbs the stairs. It's a bit of an effort for him, and we wait until he's about halfway up before starting after him.

Emma pokes me. "Look at the wallpaper," she whispers.

It's very subtle, but where the old man passes, the walls brighten—another example of his ghostly aura extending beyond his frail frame and affecting everything around him as he moves through the house.

When he gets to the top of the stairs, he heads into a bedroom. When *we* get to the top, I look with distaste at the large hole in the wall, almost expecting a couple of skeletons to climb out. The idea of poking around in there doesn't exactly fill me with excitement, but we're going to have to do it.

Not just yet, though.

We huddle in the bedroom doorway. Bertie's in there, shuffling past what we can see of a bed. Only the closest part of it is visible to us, and even that disappears when he veers toward the far corner of the room.

"What's he doing?" Mia whispers.

Ben gives a quiet snort. "Do you really think I have any clue whatsoever?"

The old man is acting even more mysteriously now. Leaning on a sturdy chair that's draped with clothes, he carefully drops to one knee, then both, and crawls into the corner of the room. There's a ghostly section of thick carpet under him, and he tugs at the edge, peeling it away from the wall.

He fumbles with a loose floorboard. It's a short section about ten inches long, and removing it reveals a neat little hideyhole. He carefully stows the journal into the recess.

As we're standing there gawking, Bertie replaces the floorboard, flattens the carpet over it, and spends the next half-minute groaning as he climbs to his feet.

"No more!" he gasps, looking at the ceiling. "No more. I'm too old for this."

He stumbles toward us, muttering under his breath. We step aside and let him pass.

"Infernal house," he grumbles. "It's just a matter of time, you know. The city's got wind of you now. They'll send inspectors to look at your wiring, your plumbing, your gas lines, *everything*. Not to mention your black mold!"

"Is he talking to the house?" Mia whispers.

Ben shrugs. "Sure sounds that way."

Bertie Sharpe heads for the stairs. "I can't legally have tenants here now, do you know that? But I need the money. Do you understand? Pah! Of course you don't."

Once again, he ignores the hole in the wall. As he gets near, his ghostly influence causes it to close, but then it reopens when he's clear.

"I'm telling you," he goes on, "if you don't let workmen in to fix the place up, it'll be condemned and shut down. And then where will you be? Eh? Where will *we* be?"

As he reaches the staircase, he pauses to shake his fist.

"Ha! All these years, all these people you've silenced, and in the end it'll be some faulty wiring and mold that shuts you down for good! Well, it serves you right. I've a good mind to burn you to the ground! Ha! What do you think about *that*?"

There's a sudden rumbling under our feet, and when I reach for the wall, the vibrations leap up my arm. An earthquake? Is it real, or part of this vision? Judging by the expressions on my friends' faces, they have no clue either.

Bertie Sharpe jerks suddenly, teetering on the edge of the top step as he clutches at his chest.

"No!" he gasps. "I didn't mean it—!"

And, to our horror, he pitches forward and topples down the staircase.

Emma twists around and clamps her hands over her ears. I'm already looking away, too. The sounds of the old man thudding down the stairs are too real and awful without seeing it as well.

Thankfully, the scene abruptly ends. The deep rumbling and ghostly glows fade.

We're left standing in silence and darkness, our flashlight beams trembling. The dusty old bones are inside the wall opposite, waiting for us to reach in and pull them out.

And it seems like the ghosts of the house are united on this, including Bertie Sharpe himself.

As if to remind us, Mr. Clydesdale roars up the stairs at us. "WHERE'S MY MATILDA?"

Chapter 17
The Journal

We huddle together by the hole in the wall.

"Shall we?" Ben says, sounding exactly like he wants us all to say no and drag him away.

"It's just some old bones, right?" I tell him.

"Go on, then, Nathaniel," Mia says, giving me a shove.

Suddenly, it's me who's standing nearest to the pitch-black recess. The others have stepped backward.

My flashlight picks out bones covered in dust and cobwebs. I can see the curve of a skull.

Breathing hard, I swallow and back off. "Look, I know we don't exactly have a choice, but . . . I mean, like Mia said, it's probably illegal to touch them, right?"

None of us have any idea if that's true, but it sounds plausible, at least in homicide cases.

"But if we leave them alone," Ben says quietly, "then we're stuck here."

Mia sighs. "Nate, you should have called the police after all."

"Huh? You said—"

"I know what I said," she snaps. "But whether we move these bones or not, the police have to know. So, if we're going to call them anyway—"

"Ah," Ben says, "but I was going to call them *anonymously*. Big difference. I hoped we'd get out of this mess, go home to bed, and then in the morning find a phone and put in an anonymous tip. The police come out here, find the bones, and we're in the clear. Win-win."

"Do you think the ghosts will keep us here all night?" Emma says. "Maybe when the sun comes up, the ghosts will fade away, and we can hurry home before our parents crawl out of bed."

That makes me feel better. "I like that plan! We just have to wait. I have comics. We can sit downstairs and read for a few hours."

Emma nods and smiles.

Ben looks around. "So we wait it out?"

Mia frowns. "We're seriously going to sit around until morning because we're too chicken to touch some old bones?"

I give her a gentle push toward the hole in the wall. "Be my guest."

She grimaces and bats my hand away. "Fine, we'll wait. But if the ghosts still don't budge when the sun comes up . . ."

In an effort to change the subject and get some distance from the skeletons, I hurry into Bertie's bedroom. "I just remembered! Let's see if that journal's still there."

Judging by the soft gasps, I'm guessing none of them have even considered that. Sometimes I think *I'm* the real brains of this operation.

Still, even I'm surprised when I pry up the short length of floorboard in the corner and find Bertie's journal. I remove it carefully, afraid it will crumble into dust even though it's only been here untouched for a year.

"I can't believe this," Emma whispers. "Hurry up and open it!"

So, kneeling in the corner, with the others leaning over my shoulders and their flashlight beams pointing at the book, I open it to the first page. The writing is in large, scrawling letters.

"My name is Albert Theodore Sharpe. If you're reading this, then I'm probably dead."

"Good start," Mia murmurs. "Exciting, catchy. It hooks the reader."

"Shh," Ben complains.

There's more on the first page. "I didn't believe in ghosts until I bought this old house in 1971," I read aloud. "I started seeing them right away. No wonder the place was so cheap—nobody else wanted it! It turns out that people died here. Lots of people. I don't scare easy, so I'm not afraid of ghosts, but . . . the house has a mind of its own.

"I'm going to write this journal as a record of what's happening while I'm living here, starting with Matilda and her husband earlier this month. That wasn't me. Of course, nobody will believe a word of this, so I'm not saying anything to the authorities. But one day, when I'm gone, and this old house is empty, maybe someone will find the bones and this journal."

Flipping a page, I lick my lips and continue.

"September 13, 1971. Janitors like me don't make much, and they've been cutting my hours, so I'm having trouble making ends meet. I figured a tenant was the answer, so I put an ad in the paper and got a response from a lady named Matilda.

"She was from out of town and seemed nice enough. Paid me a month's advance rent and moved straight in. But she waited until she was settled before telling me her husband would be out of prison next month. She had the nerve to ask if he could move in, too.

"I told her sure, but the rent is double. Two people, two rooms, right? She said, 'But he's my husband! He can share mine!' And I told her, 'No way, Missy—separate rooms only! This ain't no hotel, this is my *house*, and I live here as well.'

"She wasn't happy about that at all, and I told her she could leave if she wanted, and she said fine, she would. And then she asked for her money back. I was completely within my rights to keep the money. Rent isn't refundable. She paid in advance for a month, and the terms state one month's notice if you want to leave. So I kept her money, and she flew off the handle.

"She told me she'd report me for extortion! What a firecracker. Not the nice young lass I thought she was. And then she went on about the state of the house and how it wasn't fit to rent out anyway. Said it was illegal for landlords to rent such a dangerous place and threatened to report me to the city inspectors. Even took me upstairs and pointed out the black mold in the hallway. Ha! Like I wasn't aware already. There I was, in the middle of ripping out the wall for that very reason! It was a leaky water pipe getting into the insulation. Anyway, she complained about it, and I lost my temper and . . .

"Here's the thing. You won't believe this, but there was a rumbling, like an earthquake, and this woman, Matilda, died on the spot. Nobody else in town reported an earthquake. It's like the house got angry and stopped her heart. Yeah, I know, it's crazy. But she clutched her chest and keeled over. A young, healthy, pretty black woman with her whole life ahead of her, dead as a doornail at the top of the stairs.

"I should have called 9-1-1, but I couldn't. How would it have looked? And she was right, the house isn't fit to rent. So I put her in the wall and pretended like nothing had happened . . ."

Mia puts a hand on my shoulder. "You okay?"

My hands are shaking, my voice trembling. "Just excited to get some answers," I reply. "This was her, guys. The woman in the wall."

"We know," Ben says. "And I'm betting the next page is all about her husband knocking on the door."

It was, too. I read aloud in amazement.

"September 29, 1971. As I feared, Matilda's ex-convict husband showed up last night. Stood outside yelling for her, then broke in through the front door. He brought an axe! I wasn't about to confront him, so I hid, and he went from room to room, shouting for me, shouting for his Matilda, banging his axe on the wall, threatening to kill me and tell the police. The man's a lunatic. *Was* a lunatic. Like his wife before him, he died of a heart attack as soon as he'd stomped his way up the stairs. Dropped dead outside my bedroom.

"It was like the house had waited for him, and I'm glad, because it would have been hellish trying to drag him anywhere. He died right next to the wall where I'd put his wife, so I just had to open it up again and stuff him inside as well.

"The smell was horrible. But I hadn't really noticed any bad smells until I opened it up, so I figured it would be all right long-term for the two of them. I put the sheetrock back up, sealed the joints, repainted, and that was that.

"You have to be wondering if I felt guilty. Well, yes and no. When I went to work or into town, I felt bad. When I came home, I didn't. Took me a while to realize that the house wraps me up in a blanket of safety and reassurance. Yes, it sounds crazy, but I think it needs me, so it tries to take away any feelings of guilt. It works, too. So yeah, while I'm living here, I have this strong feeling everything's going to be all right and I shouldn't feel bad, that nobody will miss an ex-convict except for his parole officer . . ."

I have a quick flip through the pages. I reckon we're already halfway through what he's written.

"January 1, 1972. Nobody ever came by to find Matilda and her husband. No police, no parole officers, nobody. Looks like everything's going to work out. I don't feel great about it, which is why I'm keeping this journal going. I need the money, and I have a new tenant coming by next week. Things are going to work out okay . . ."

My hands are shaking much harder now. When I thumb through the remaining pages, it's clear there's a distinct pattern.

"The entries get shorter and shorter," I croak. "December 13, 1979, Janie Tompkinson, buried under the deck. August 8, 1984, David Stevens, buried in the backyard, built summer house over the grave. It's a list of the dead, one name per page, with a date." I'm aware my voice is rising, becoming a strangled squawk. "Look how many pages there are! All these people, all killed in this house and buried in—"

"WHERE'S MY MATILDA?" a man's voice booms from behind us.

We all yell and spin around. Mr. Clydesdale stands there, brandishing the axe. This time I fear he's actually going to use it on us, because his ghostly patience must be at an end by now.

He stomps into the room. The four of us press our backs to the wall—not the smartest strategy, but common sense tends to desert us when faced with death.

"Okay, okay!" Ben yells. "We were just reading up about you, that's all!"

I brandish the journal as proof. "Yeah, see? We understand now. So many people! You just want closure, and we can help with that. Let us pass so we can get on with the job."

"Or so we can run straight downstairs and out the front door," Mia mutters.

The rest of us glance at her.

Ben whispers, "I like that plan better. But nobody gets left behind this time. Okay?"

We quickly agree.

Mr. Clydesdale is a fearsome figure, and the yellow eyes make him look demonic as he stomps toward us with murder in mind. But I feel sorry for him, too. And his wife, and all those other people the house has claimed over the years. This has to end.

Still . . .

We're Darkseekers, and we investigate the paranormal around our spooky town of Darkhill. No ghostly tale is too unbelievable. We *know* ghosts exist, and though we're afraid of them, we'll confront them anyway.

But lifting bones from a wall?

Sorry. Not our job.

"RUN!" Ben yells.

Chapter 18
A Bone to Pick

We can hardly believe our luck

All four of us escape the grasping hands of the huge man. Correction—*one* grasping hand. The other grips the axe, which for once is a blessing.

We hurtle past the hole in the wall and stampede down the stairs, almost falling over each other. Mr. Clydesdale thunders after us, roaring over and over about his wife.

The front door is clear—but not for long. The Victorian lady appears out of thin air. The 1940s youth fades into view next to her. The electrician, the black-suited man with the dark glasses, and at least two dozen more, one by one, winking into existence to form a crowded, impenetrable wall that stretches down the hall.

Gasping with terror, we skid to a halt at the foot of the stairs and huddle together, glancing back to see Mr. Clydesdale almost upon us.

I honestly think they've lost all confidence in us and want to drag us down to the underworld where they can beat on us forevermore. I can't help thinking of Bertie Sharpe dealing with these ghosts for decades. The house would kill people, and he'd have to bury them somewhere about the property, and then their ghosts would return to torment *him*. I can almost understand how he grew so numb over the years, dispatching them again and again in numerous different ways, becoming callous about it, even laughing . . .

I said I can *almost* understand. We're not Bertie Sharpe, and we're terrified.

"Well, it was good knowing you all," I tell my friends. "Sorry I didn't call the police like I—"

Then something totally unexpected happens.

The front door flies open.

And all the ghosts abruptly vanish.

Their glows fade and plunge everything into darkness, leaving us standing there, breathing hard, alone in the hall at the foot of the stairs, our flashlights bobbing and jerking about.

Except that now three more flashlights shine through the open door. A trio of figures stands there, looking in at us.

"Well, there they are," a familiar voice says. It's Sam Davis, and he sounds disgusted. "What a bunch of wusses. Are you peeing your pants right now? Scared of the dark, are we?"

"Poor little things," Kaley says with a giggle. "Look at their white faces!" She raises her voice to us. "You look like you've seen a ghost!"

Ben finds his own voice. "We have," he croaks. "What are you doing here?"

I realize I might have forgotten to mention something. "Oh, uh . . . Ben, you know when I said I didn't call the police? Well, I called these guys instead."

Mia's flashlight whips around to dazzle me. "You did *what*?"

I'm embarrassed, but at the same time, I'm astonished and over the moon. My plan actually worked! These three are mostly strangers to the house, and the spirit world is still shy around them. Sam, Kaley, and Austin showed up, threw open the door, and the ghosts vanished.

"Yes," I tell my friends with a grin, "I called them. Guys, the Hauntstalkers are taking over the night shift. Time for us to go home!"

While I'm ushering the others toward the door before a legion of ghosts return, the curious but woefully ignorant Hauntstalkers step inside.

"Hey," Austin barks, stopping us dead. "You said there are bones somewhere. Was that a lie?"

"Nope," I tell him. "They're upstairs. You'll see the hole in the wall. But I would leave them there until the police arrive. In fact, honestly, you shouldn't stay here at all. We were about to die before you showed up. I hate to admit it, but you saved our lives."

"Oh, that's right, tons of ghosts trapped you in the house," Sam sneers as he begins to wander down the hall. "Well, how about you let the Hauntstalkers see if we can spot any spectral figures or apparitions."

It's not that Sam, Kaley, and Austin don't believe us. They probably do. But seeing is believing, and I don't think they truly appreciate the scale of the situation, otherwise they would be fleeing instead of heading so casually toward the nearest room.

"It's not just a couple of ghosts," I tell them. "It's, like, *dozens*. There's a journal upstairs—"

With a start, I realize the journal isn't upstairs at all. It's still clutched in my sweaty hand. I think my fingertips have left indentations on the cover.

I hurry after Sam and thrust the dusty book at him. "Look. Proof! This was Bertie Sharpe's. He wrote detailed notes about the first two victims, and then listed the rest."

"They weren't the first," Emma says softly.

I glance at her. "Okay, the first two who died while Bertie Sharpe was living here. But there were plenty more before he owned the place."

"What?" Kaley exclaims. "You're saying the previous owner was a murderer, too? You're lying again."

"It wasn't the owners that killed people," I urge. "It was the house. The house has been doing it for a hundred years! There's a Victorian lady—"

"Enough!" Austin snaps. "Look."

We all fall silent. Almost without realizing it, we've ended up in the living room. The rocking chair is creaking back and forth.

My first thought is that Austin is tugging on the length of string. But two seconds later, I'm convinced otherwise. None of the Hauntstalkers are moving. Nor are the Darkseekers. We're all just standing there, gawking at the rocking chair as it creaks back and forth on its own.

"O-*kay*," Kaley says, taking a step back. "And nobody's doing that? Guys?"

"Not me," Sam mutters.

Austin holds something up in his hand and points his flashlight at it. It's the string—but it's limp, hanging straight down. "It's none of us."

There's a long silence. Then Mia says, "Time to go, guys. NOW!"

Her command makes all of us jump, and we hustle out of the room and along the hallway. The front door is wide open, but I have an awful feeling it's about to slam shut, and we'll be plunged into the realm of ghosts once more . . .

To my relief, we all spill out the door onto the deck, then down the steps.

"Nate, your stuff!" Ben exclaims.

Panic shoots through me. My backpack! My camcorder! My comics! "Yeah, good call," I say, turning toward the house. "Uh . . . stay here."

A bunch of cheap candles aren't important, but everything else is. My backpack is in the upstairs hallway, propped against the wall.

Never in my life have I rushed up a flight of stairs so quickly. I feel like dozens of phantoms are watching me closely, conferring, trying to decide when to leap out of hiding again. They will, too, as soon as they're over whatever oddball shyness they have of newcomers.

To my surprise, my backpack has spilled open. Grumbling, I shove comics in as fast as I can, scoop up chocolate bars, check the camcorder's not lost, grab the lighter from the floor at the last second, and turn to run.

Mr. Clydesdale is standing there, blocking my escape.

"No," I moan.

He glowers at me. But he doesn't start ranting about Matilda this time. Instead, he seems oddly fixated on my right hand.

"What?" I croak. "Please don't kill me! Look, I promise we'll tell the police everything as soon as we leave, and then they'll come and tear this place apart. They'll find the bones, and . . ."

Though his eyes are glowing yellow, it's clear he's still interested in what I'm holding. Slowly, I turn my hand palm upwards.

"It's just a lighter," I mumble.

Bertie Sharpe appears suddenly. He's a faint apparition, only visible for a second as he shakes his fist at the ceiling and shouts, "I've a good mind to burn you to the ground!"

Then he's gone.

Mr. Clydesdale lifts his eerie gaze to meet mine. The meaning is clear.

"No," I whisper. "No, I can't do that. You want me to . . . to what? Start a fire? Burn the house down? No way!"

Ben yells up the stairs. "NATE! Hurry up!"

But Mr. Clydesdale isn't budging.

Figures fade into existence. Others step out from the shadows. Suddenly, I'm surrounded by a silent, motionless throng of sinister dead people, all standing there glaring at me.

I have a terrible sinking feeling in my gut. It's the realization that I'm not getting out of here alive . . . *unless I start a fire.*

I go through the motions pulling a few comics out of my backpack. Not the Spookies summer special, and definitely not the amazing Rotten Buzzard issues—but maybe some of these cheap Edge of Reality stories . . .

What am I doing? There's no way I can do this. It doesn't matter that it's a wicked old house the town will be better off without. *I'm not an arsonist!* The amount of trouble I'd be in if . . . The mind boggles. I can't even imagine!

But, seeing no alternative right now, I tear pages out of my comics and scrunch them into loose balls. Before I know it, and with no other plan of action springing to mind, I'm holding the lighter to the paper. A small flame takes hold.

Don't worry, it'll fizzle out. Just light the fire and get out of here.

Actually, I'm fairly sure that's true. The pages go up in flames and burn strongly, but I think it'll be short-lived. It's not too close to the wall, and I doubt the flooring will catch anytime soon.

"There," I whisper, standing up and clutching my backpack with what's left of my comics. "It's done. Now let me go."

To my surprise, Mr. Clydesdale steps aside. Others do, too, and a path opens up—an escape route to the staircase.

"Th-thanks," I stutter.

Although my elbows bump against them as I weave my way past, the ghosts begin to fade until I'm alone in the hall.

Then an ominous rumbling fills the air. What is *that*? It feels like an earthquake!

I pause as an awful pain creeps into my chest. It grows sharper and sharper, like someone is pressing a cold knife between my ribs. Gasping, I clutch at my chest. The house! It's killing me!

"NATE!" Ben yells up the stairs. "Get down here NOW! Something's happening!"

Yeah, no kidding, my brain screams as I start to reel. Everything's beginning to spin, and my chest is exploding.

What happens next is a bit of a blur. Am I falling? Or . . . floating? Strong, invisible hands hold me upright. *Lots* of hands. I'm aware of my feet dangling, not quite touching the floor as I'm propelled the rest of the way along the hall. Then I'm flying head first down the stairs, but in slow motion, still gripped by an unseen force. The pain in my chest is agonizing.

The rumbling grows, but there's another noise as well—a rising wail, the combined shrieks of many long-dead ghosts. They're deafening, but the terrible pain in my chest abruptly eases. It's like the ghosts are locked in a unified battle of wills against the evil spirit in the house, or simply distracting it while they carry me out.

Then I'm thrown onto the deck, and the door slams shut behind me.

"Nate!" Emma yells in my ear. "Nate, what's wrong? What happened?"

"Are you all right?" Ben demands, helping me up even though I really just want to lie down. "You literally *flew* out that door!"

"What's going on in there?" Mia mutters, her attention on the house.

Sweating and shaking, I bat my friends away and rub at my chest. "We have to get out of here."

The pain has completely gone now. I don't even want to think about how close I came to death just then. I set a fire! I attacked the house, and it tried to kill me!

Sam, Kaley, and Austin haven't said much, but I can tell they're disturbed by the continued shrieking inside the house. Maybe now they'll truly believe.

"Banshees," Ben says with a vague gesture. "Warning us that someone's about to die."

I can't be bothered to explain how wrong he is. Besides, the shrieking does sound like it could be a load of banshees.

"It's over," Emma says as she thrusts my bike into my hands. "Let's go home. We'll call the police in the morning."

"Anonymously," Ben adds, climbing onto his own bike. "Got everything, Nate? Let's get the girls' bikes from the field and get out of here."

"Hey!" Sam calls. He holds up the journal and laughs. "Just so you know, this is *our* case now.

We have the evidence, okay? This is officially Hauntstalkers business. Got it?"

"That's not yours," Ben growls.

"Leave it," I whisper. Who cares, anyway? All I can think about is the small fire upstairs.

It's hard to see anyone's face in the darkness, but I can tell Austin is scowling. "*We'll* call the police first thing. You stay home. We'll be here to meet them and explain everything."

"Explain *what*?" Ben challenges him. "You have no idea—"

But Mia gently takes his arm and whispers something.

After a moment, his shoulders sag, and he gives a nod. "Fine, I guess. Whatever." He faces the Hauntstalkers again. "But if you do call the police, promise you won't say a word about us, okay? If you want to take the credit, then make sure the Darkseekers weren't here tonight *at all*."

Sam grins. "Now that's something we can agree on. It's a deal. Right, Austin?"

"Hmm," Austin mumbles.

And with that, we part ways. I take one last look at the house before it drops out of sight behind us. It stands silent now, and to my relief, I see no sign of smoke, nor the faint glow of a fire in an upstairs window.

Or . . . or do I?

"Nate, come on," Emma urges.

It's been a long night, but we're finally on our way home. We ride in silence until we reach the familiar Cold Falls subdivision sign, and then we stop behind it, out of sight in case anyone's up at this ridiculous hour of the morning.

"Well, I don't know about you, but I could sleep until lunchtime," Emma says with a yawn.

"I think we all could," Ben agrees. "But . . . don't we want to be there when those clowns meet the police? I know it'll be early, but—"

"No," I tell him with a shudder. "Ben, the ghosts made me start a fire."

All three blink at me.

"You . . . started a fire?" Emma repeats.

"I'm sure it's gone out by now, but I don't want to be anywhere near that place when the police show up. I'm going to bed."

"For once, I agree with Nathaniel," Mia says.

I sigh. "Thanks, but the name's Nate. *Why* do you always have to—"

"All right, all right," Emma says, holding her hands up. "No arguing. Let's sneak home and hope nobody has missed us yet. Night, everyone."

She rides off, and a moment later, Mia smiles and departs as well. That leaves Ben and me.

"You actually started a fire?" he asks.

I nod. "With some of my comics."

"And what else?" Ben narrows his eyes at me. "There's something you're not telling me, isn't there? You started a fire, and then there was that rumbling, and you came out as white as a ghost."

My lips are suddenly dry as I gingerly rub my chest. "Let's talk tomorrow."

Ben notices, and I think he guesses I might have had the beginnings of a heart attack earlier. Thankfully, he doesn't press me about it.

"You did good tonight, Nate. I never in a million years thought you'd have the nerve to step foot inside that house alone, never mind stay there and deal with ghosts. And there were a *lot* of ghosts. Pretty intense stuff."

"Thanks," I mumble, trying to shrug it off. But, truthfully, his praise means a lot.

All in all, this has been the most frightening night of my life. I'm glad it's over but also pleased it happened. I proved to the team that I'm not a complete waste of space who will bolt every time someone says "Boo!"

Not only that, I proved to myself that I can push through the fear. No more running off at a crucial moment!

Honestly, I don't think I'll ever again be as scared as I was tonight.

But if I am, then . . . I'll deal with it.

Epilogue

It's Sunday evening, and we're squeezed together on the sofa at Ben's house watching the local news. It's pretty shocking, actually. This story has spread across the nation.

". . . We're here in the small town of Darkhill, standing outside the blackened remains of the house where Albert Sharpe lived for fifty years."

The reporter on the TV, a redheaded woman by the name of Nancy Trace, gestures over her shoulder, where several police cars and a couple of white vans are clustered in front of the ruins. Blue lights are flashing as officers take notes, and plenty of forensic investigators walk about wearing gloves, masks, and slip-on booties.

The house is gone. Nothing left but a charred and smoking mess. I'm slightly terrified that the fire inspectors will identify the source of the fire as a pile of comics, but otherwise I feel a sense of relief. Nobody else will be in danger from the evil that lurks within the old place. And the ghosts can finally rest.

". . . After the shocking discovery of human bones among the debris in the early hours of this morning, more bodies are being unearthed throughout the property. Police have yet to make an official comment about the number of dead found thus far, but unofficial sources suggest it's well into double digits. The grisly story has caught the attention of the entire nation, and . . ."

We all lean forward. "Is that Sam Davis?" Mia gasps.

"Yup," Ben mutters.

Sam and his sister Kaley have appeared in the background as the camera pans that way. Austin is there, too. And behind them, their parents. All look grim.

Ben's dad is sitting in the armchair to our left. "You know them from school?"

"Unfortunately, yes," Emma responds.

"What on earth were they doing there so early this morning?"

"I have *no idea*," Ben says, shaking his head. "I can't even imagine."

The news reporter is interviewing them now, and Sam in particular looks pleased with himself.

"Yeah, passed by on an early-morning bike ride, saw the flames, and called 9-1-1. But while we were waiting for the fire department, we found a journal lying on the ground, and as soon as we read it, we knew we had to call Channel 9 News. The world has to know about this." He gestures to himself, then to Kaley and Austin. "We call ourselves the Hauntstalkers, and we've been investigating the Bertie Sharpe rumors for some time. Now, thanks to us, the mystery of all these missing people is solved, and their families will finally get some closure."

Mia scoffs openly. "Nice speech, doofus! I bet he spent all night preparing that."

"He's right, though," Ben's dad says. "That journal's quite a find."

"They're idiots," Ben mutters.

Nancy Trace turns to the camera. "Forensic anthropologists believe some of the bones date back to the 1950s, twenty years *before* Bertie Sharpe bought the house, and perhaps even earlier than that, giving rise to speculation that Mr. Sharpe was not responsible for the deaths. Police are analyzing the journal as we speak, and all of this is yet to be confirmed. It may be weeks before we know the facts of this case, especially as the house is nothing more than a smoking ruin. One thing's for sure: this shocking discovery further darkens the shadow hanging over an already sinister town. This is Nancy Trace of Channel 9 News, reporting from Darkhill."

"Well, I'm glad the house burned down," Ben says. "Nobody in their right mind would ever buy it anyway."

His mom has been listening from the doorway. "What an awful mess."

"What's *really* awful," Mia says, "is how much attention the Hauntstalkers are going to get now. Did you see how proud they all looked? And their parents didn't seem too upset, either."

"Probably all kinds of multimillion-dollar book deals and high-paying interviews lined up," I tell her. "Looks like they got lucky."

Ben's mom grimaces. "I'd hate that kind of attention. I'm so glad you kids weren't involved. What a horrible thing! Promise me you won't go sifting through the burnt-out rubble of that house or anything crazy like that."

It's not a lie when Ben says, "We absolutely promise not to go anywhere near that house at any point in the future."

"No way," Emma says.

"Not gonna happen," Mia agrees.

Then Ben's mom looks at me with raised eyebrows. "Nate?"

I spread my hands and put on my very best innocent expression. "Seriously? Do you even know me? Do I seem like the sort of person who would set foot in a house like that?"

She smiles. "Well, I suppose not."

So, the Hauntstalkers are famous now, thanks to me. But that's okay, I suppose. We'd wanted fame as well, at first, but not if it means being grounded for life.

Oh well. We Darkseekers will just have to continue investigating the paranormal in our own way, which is quietly, thoroughly . . .

And, above all, *fearlessly.*

Darkhill Scary Stories

Ben, Emma, Nate, and Mia are determined to film the paranormal in the creepy town of Darkhill. They call themselves DARKSEEKERS. And there's an abundance of spooky stuff where they live!

Written by the author of the Island of Fog books, this supernatural series is perfect for those who love Goosebumps.

Find out release dates of future Darkseeker adventures at darkhillbooks.com.

Printed in Great Britain
by Amazon

18700024R00103